I0682161

WEIRD TRAILS
THE MAGAZINE OF SUPERNATURAL COWBOY STORIES

April 1933 issue

Published by Wildside Press
www.wildsidepress.com

THE MAGAZINE OF SUPERNATURAL COWBOY STORIES

Vol XX   No 1

Published monthly by Bar Sinister Publications, 13 Boot Hill Drive, Tombstone Arizona. Entered as second-class matter April 20, 1923 at the post office in Tombstone Arizona, under the act of March 3, 1879. Single copies cost what we can get for them. Subscriptions, well fergit it, you gotta be kiddin'. Publishers are not responsible for the loss of unsolicited manuscripts or the sanity of those submitting them, although every care will be taken of such material while in their possession. The contents of this publication are fully protected by copyright and must not be reproduced either wholly or in part unless you want a .45 slug between your beady little eyeballs.

DURANGO FEAR editor emeritus   GEORGE SCITHERS production manager
ABNER GIBBER editor   DIANE WEINSTEIN cowgirl
DARRELL SCHWEITZER managing editor   JOE PUMILIA & BILL WALLACE instigators

CONTENTS FOR APRIL, 1933

The HAUNTED CORRAL

Howdy, all you owlhoots, outlaws, and outer ones! With this here issue *Weird Trails* enters its tenth full year of publication. And what a ride it's been so far! Why just the other day, as we relaxed at his ranch over whiskey and roast shoggoth (which comes out more like a pudding than a steak, admittedly), our illustrious Founding Editor and still Editor Emeritus, Durango Fear remarked, "You know Abner, I thought you'd have gone mad by now."

And we responded, "How can you tell?"

"Got a point, son," he said in that long drawl of his.

Indeed, there have been some mighty *weird* things a'goin' on around the editorial offices these past ten years. Like the time a large, rather suspicious-smelling parcel arrived in the mail, and when we opened it, there was what appeared to be a human head inside. Imagine our surprise when its eyes snapped opened and a gravelly voice said, "Arr . . . matey, be ye pirates then? Just don't ye go mistakin' me for a cannonball and we'll get along fine."

Clearly the mailman had done misdelivered a parcel intended for *Sodden Sargasso Sea Stories,* which used to be located down the hall. But that magazine had been out of business now for several years; and, indeed, the whole east wing of the building had since collapsed into a shapeless mass of mildew and mold. What could we do with our unexpected guest then? Durango, who was still in charge in those days, was completely unperturbed. He removed the bandanna our guest was wearing, substituted a Stetson, and set him to work reading manuscripts. Our new editorial assistant worked out quite well, once he'd learned to turn the pages with his teeth. True, he does tend to mark his editorial comments with drool, but we can't imagine that any of our *Weird Trails* regulars could possibly object to *that.*

We *could* tell you about the chittering, winged, crab-like Things which descended upon us one night and attempted to remove our brains . . . but suffice it to say that *Weird Trails* is popular even on Yuggoth, and our assailants were quickly mollified with free back-issues and a subscription — though how exactly we are to send copies to other planets has never been clear. Meanwhile, we send them to a post office box in Brattleboro, Vermont.

Then there was the case of the unsolicited submission so ghastly that it really *did* begin to crawl up our leg, and could only be laid to rest by a quick

A Jimmy Pipe o' Peace

PRINCE ALBERT

the national joy smoke

has put the "Indian Sign" on all the tongue-broiling, smartweed brands. P. A. can't bite *your* tongue nor any man's, patented process removes the sting.

Sold everywhere in 5c bags, 10c tins, pound and half-pound humidors.

R. J. REYNOLDS TOBACCO CO.
Winston-Salem, N. C.

PRINCE ALBERT

CRIMP CUT
LONG BURNING PIPE AND
CIGARETTE TOBACCO

spell from *Webster's Desktop Necronomicon* and a rejection slip through the heart, but we editors are used to that sort of thing.

Mad? Never. We're not even irate, though some of our readers seem to be, such as **Zango P. Oakley** from Dead Mule Oklahoma, who writes:

Dear Editor, What in tarnation do you think that you're doing with my favorite magazine? "Blazing Sixguns of Slavering Horror" by Captain S.P. Meek USA (an' what the hell kinda cowboy name is "Captain Meek" and what was he captain of?) was complete horse-puckey, particularly the part where the hero (?) shoots the old Injun shaman seven times between the eyes before the Injun breaks down into a mass of putrescent ooze and starts singing Broadway show tunes. Fer one thing, didn't the hero read the title of his own story? And fer another, I seen some mighty peculiar Injuns in these here parts — from the Whateley tribe, mostly, a surly bunch that come from back East a couple generations ago — and it stands to reason you can't shoot a man (I use the term loosely) between the eyes seven times unless he's got eight eyes, and I never seen a Whateley that had more than four, not countin' the ones around the waist which look more like extra belly-buttons and ain't good fer much. So this Meek feller just don't know what he's talkin' about. I bet he's done all his "research" in books, rather than out here in the West, where life is lived in the raw and men are men, and Things are Things.

An' I ain't ever heard an Injun sing a Broadway show-tune. It ain't natural!

In fact the only thing I liked about your January issue was the non-Euclidean cover art. My wife and eighteen of the kids disappeared into strange angles while a-starin' at it. Makes for fewer mouths to feed.

By contrast **Orlin Hangdeeble** of North Nyarlathotep, Nova Scotia, seems much more pleased with us:

Wow! What a great issue! It's true that I've never been west of the western-most window of the attic in which my family, ashamed of my peculiar habits, sealed me up shortly after my birth, but still I dream of the Great Outdoors and the American West, which your magazine brings to me so vividly each and every month — by means I am not entirely at liberty to disclose, and I strongly deny that the unusually high incidence of handless or armless postmen in the local region has anything to do with me. "Blazing Sixguns of Slavering Horror" by Captain S.P. Meek was the most convincing story I've read in your pages since M.M. Moamrath's "Showdown at Fuggoth Flats" back in '28 or so. I could all but taste that mysterious shaman dissolving into ooze, and more than anything else I wanted to know what show tunes he was singing, but I suppose the author has to leave some things out to create suspense and suggest more than he actually delivers. But darn! That one was a corker! I also like the new Ron Goulart serial, "Trouble At Cthulhu Canyon." Sheriff Jim Destiny has always been a favorite, ever since "Guns of the Shambler" appeared in your fine pages.

I particularly appreciated the non-Euclidean artwork. Maybe if I stare at it just so, I will be able to pay your editorial offices a visit sometime soon.

We are always pleased to hear from real Western readers for the insight they give into genuine Western lore and folkways, such as the following from **D. Ceased,** of Whynot, Wyoming:

Dear Sir, your January issue certainly had a powerful effect on the boys here at the Bar-Nothing Ranch. They got into such an argument over which story was best, that the only way to settle the matter, according to the Code of the West, was for each man to carve the title of his favorite story on a .45 bullet and then have it out in the middle of the dusty street at high noon with anybody who disagreed with him. Subsequent autopsies produced the following ratings of the stories:

1) "Trouble in Cthulhu Canyon" (part 1) by Ron Goulart.

2) "Blazing Sixguns of Slavering Horror" by Captain S.P. Meek, USA.

3) "The Buffalo's Revenge" by Arthur J. Burks.

4) "O Dat Golden Ichor" by Petronius Drumgoole.

5) "Trail of the Turgid Terror" by Zealia Bishop.

6) "Thundering Brains" (conclusion) by Oliver Osgood Oblongata.

7) "The Whispering Wazoo" by Roman Ranieri.

Admittedly the lengths gone to obtain these ratings might have left us shorthanded here on the ranch, if I hadn't found a very helpful advertisement in your fine companion magazine, Exciting Zombie Adventures. After a short trip to Haiti for the bunch of us, all our problems have been solved.

You oughta try blowing your brains out sometime. It gives you a whole new perspective.

A would-be writer, **Tarasacodissa von Chang** asks for advice:

Dear Editor, I notice that in pulp-paper magazines such as your own, persons of minority ethnicities, particularly when depicted as villains, are often referred to by such short-hand terms as Dagoes, Chinks, Japs, Frogs, wetbacks, etc. Since I myself am part Mexican, part Chinese, part Lapp, part Berber, part Visigothic, part Hottentot, part Apache, part Blackfellow, part Eskimo, part Irish, part Albanian, and there was a red-skinned great-grandmother on my father's side of the family who laid eggs, how do you think I ought to deal with such matters in my own fiction without bringing angry relatives down on my head?

Avoid ethnic slurs. Enunciate.

And finally, another letter from a real Old-Timer of the West, **T. "Tex" Phundament** of Zamboanga Springs, Colorado:

Dear Editor, I truly appreciated the feature on "Eldritch Cowboy Songs" in your January 1933 issue. I wish you had expounded a bit more on the "hideously noxious fragment" quoted by the gentleman from Rhode Island. I heard a version of it as a child myself, back in '50 or so, and could still sing it loud and clear if I weren't afraid of what it might do to the horses, not to mention my neighbors. Why, I knew a man once who recited a limerick which rhymed "Cthulhu" whilst in a pass high up in the Rockies. Brought down an avalanche on his whole party. No survivors. It was almost as if Nature herself wanted to shut him up. You may reasonably ask, then how anybody knows what happened? Yes, you might. Didn't Mr. Moamrath write about that once? Yes:

He vanished in snow
they asked wendigo
and never again was he sawn.

But I am afraid an old cowboy sometimes rambles. I think I can safely write out the lyrics in question:

Down in the West Texas town
    of Eldritcho,
I fell in love with a scaly-faced thing.
All through the night
    we would gibber by starlight,
waiting for doom
    that the Old Ones would bring.

Black the abysses
    I saw in her eyes then,
black was her heart
    and wicked her spell,
when I caught her one night
    in a pit with a shoggoth,
I won't say what I did
    but I sent them to Hell.

There is more, Mr. Editor, but even I don't dare set it down on paper. Can't you see the hideous threat against all mankind implied by those lyrics? You don't think the hero of the song got away with it that easily, do you? It's why I moved away from Texas. Every word of it, like every word of every story in Weird Trails *is true!*

It's true that the people in West Texas have interbred with gigantic, hideously intelligent, cosmic armadillos for generations now, and that the little armadillos we see in the desert are the messengers and spies of the Old Ones. Back east they've got little critters called "sowbugs" that live under rocks, and they look like armadillos too, no bigger'n your fingernail, but they're spies too, and they're on to those of us that know the truth! But no one will believe me, that armadillos are just waiting for all of mankind to vanish through some of the non-Euclidean angles of the illustrations in some pulp magazine — Say, Mr. Editor, which side are you on, anyway? You ain't got scales, do you? [Only bathroom scales — Ed.] *— so they can reclaim the Earth as their own.*

Which leads me to the main question I have to ask you in all seriousness: if the world ends and the armadillos take over, can I get the rest of my subscription refunded?

Only if you're around to collect.

We also heard from **Alonzo Argh** of East Artichoke Arkansas, who says that his main ambition in life is to publish letters in magazines like this one. Alas, we have run out of room and can't fit in his letter, but we are certain he will achieve his goal if he persists.

THE MOST POPULAR STORY
Reader voting for the January issue was voluminous and hotly contested, even discounting such events as what happened on the Bar Nothing Ranch in Wyoming.

First place went to Part One of "Trouble At Cthulhu Canyon" by the ever-popular Ron Goulart.

Second place, by a narrow margin, went to the controversial "Blazing Sixguns of Slavering Horror" by Captain S.P. Meek, USA.

How I Learned JUJITSU
In 30 Minutes
And My Sensational Experience In Using It

By Kirtland Bowen

"KIRT, I'm a Pink-eyed Hyena if that fellow weighed more than 125 pounds! Yet the little cuss made big 'Tubby' Williams seem like a paralyzed hippopotamus!"

This was but part of the highly colored description Steve Clark gave me of the match at the Athletic Club the night before. But the whole story certainly struck a responsive chord in me. As a matter of fact any story in which a little fellow got the better of a bigger and stronger man always had an extraordinary fascination for me.

"I scouted up this 'Up-to-date David' after the match," continued Steve. "And I asked him how he was able to turn the trick on 'Tubby!' He said he had merely used a couple of Jujitsu tricks he'd picked up. I asked him where he learned the course given by some Captain Smith. And Kirt, he claims he mastered the fundamental secrets of Jujitsu from this course in a half hour! What do you know about that?"

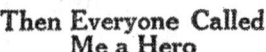

I found myself in the center of a hero-worshipping crowd

It wasn't entirely this enthusiastic story of Steve's that prompted me to send for Captain Smith's course. The real reason was that as long as I could remember, every one had always made me conscious of the fact that I was undersized—made me feel that they thought I was only a near-man, incapable of taking a real man's part. Gad, it sure used to make me rave! But if this Jujitsu was what it was cracked up to be, I felt that I had found the solution.

So the very night after I received the set of illustrated lessons, I started to read them. I found to my amazement, that Captain Smith was "The Captain Smith" who had been Chief Jujitsu Instructor in the U. S. Army during the war. And I hadn't gone far before I decided that he certainly knew how to teach Jujitsu. He explained his own Master Secret of Jujitsu, The Stahara, and around that he taught a wonderful collection of these weird Jap tricks and holds. And the whole interesting system was as simple as A B C—full of illustrations and definite instructions for every trick.

Mastered Secret In 30 Minutes

Well just for the sport of it, I timed myself. And would you believe it! IT WAS LESS THAN 30 MINUTES before I had mastered his Stahara secret and was able to apply it! Then the sparks began to fly. I called Dad into my bedroom, and you should have seen the expression on his face when I floored him! And believe me, Dad is no cripple—he weighs about 180.

I don't know why I wasn't fired out of my own home. Guess I would have been if Dad hadn't become converted to the wonderful system. As it was, every second we had off, we got together for what we called our "Jujitsu Workout." And it sure was some sport! It also put us in the pink of condition. As weeks went by, I could almost feel myself get harder and more vigorous. And "pep"—Oh Boy! I found I could do fully twice as much work and still feel fresh as a daisy.

Well it was about a week ago that I had a chance to give my Jujitsu a real test. Dot Hadley had invited me to a reception given at her club. I liked Dot a lot, though I always felt that she, too, classed me as a poor apology for a man.

It was shortly after eleven, I think, when the interruption came. I had been "sitting out" the dance to have a smoke when I saw Dot come out of the ladies' dressing room. She was so deathly pale that I jumped to my feet.

"I think there are burglars in the dressing room. I'm going to get some of the boys."

I felt myself redden. "Get some of the boys." So Dot couldn't think of me as a man. I rushed to the dressing room, behind the portieres, I collided with somebody. A huge ugly looking brute swore in a low voice.

"Listen you damn little shrimp, if you open your face . . ."

He started for me—some sort of blackjack in his hand.

I was astonished—not at his move but at my own coolness in the face of such danger. A cold calculating personality seemed to have replaced my formerly normal nervous self.

It all seemed like a regular morning practise with Dad. The lightning-like parry. The sharp return jab. An unconscious shifting towards his rear. A quick twist, using the Stahara, and I was applying Captain Smith's famous Deathlock. He was powerless.

Then Everyone Called Me a Hero

I was first conscious of the presence of the others when I found myself in the center of a hero-worshipping crowd. Dot was crying one minute and laughing the next. For the first time in my life I felt like an honest-to-goodness movie hero.

But aside from this small-town satisfaction I feel that my experience with Jujitsu has been priceless. Certainly, I shall never be troubled by people thinking I cannot take a man's part—if you notice a ring on Dot's finger, you'll know that she certainly feels otherwise. Then in addition to keeping me in perfect trim, it has given me self-confidence, poise, and a keener brain. I am absolutely convinced that the raise which my employer recently gave me is due to my improvement from my Jujitsu training.

No man or woman should be without this famous Jujitsu Training of Captain Smith's. Prominent professional and business men throughout the country believe it cannot be beaten as a body-builder and means of defence. Among these are such famous athletes as Benny Leonard, Lightweight Champion of the World, and Lieut. Oliphant, famous All-American Star, and such men as Eli Swaveley, Principal of the Army and Navy Preparatory School.

When I sent for my course, I was impressed with the fair offer made by the Stahara Publishing Company, who publish Capt. Smith's Jujitsu training. You have the entire course sent to you absolutely free without any obligations. After five days, if you are not absolutely delighted you can send it back and you will owe nothing. But if you find like I did that it's the only thing for keeping you fit, and giving you an effective weapon for defence, then you can keep the course, and send only $5. It's a sort of "heads you win, tails the other fellow loses" proposition, so I'd advise you to send for the training before this offer is withdrawn.

KIRTLAND BOWEN.

RIDERS OF THE PURPLE OOZE

by M.M. Moamrath

illustrated by Ed Ward

The squamous lunary sphere gibbered its leprous beams over the shambling Apache village under the hideous overhanging dewlap of the mesa, just past the arroyo where Dead Man's Creek is wont to gurgle after spring rains. The angular shadows of the *tipis* and *wigwams* seemed to slumber abhorrently in the necrophilious illumination. In the distance perverted coyotes howled at the waning sun nameless chants that were old when mankind was only worms squirming on the shores of the Permean sea. Elsewhere across the plains, normal coyotes howled nameless chants at the rising moon.

It was into this dread scenario that Buck Eldritch came riding on his cayuse, in his saddle bags an Apache transliteration of the dreaded *Negrognomicon* of the insane Bantu pygmy medicine man, Bundolo Kreegah. He hoped he wouldn't have to use it. He had learned from Capt. Jedidiah Gibber at Fort Archaic that Jake "Wild Willie" Cryptos was stirring up the Apaches with some sort of bull sweat about the return of the old Indian Elderly Gods, but it was the opinion of Sheriff Swiftie Thanatops that there might be something in that talk of aetherial powers after all.

"After all," Thanatops had allowed as they sipped suds at the Long Branch, "my grandma was part Mescalero and some of the tales she told me made my hair spin."

Buck was here to find out the truth. Little did Thanatops know that Buck was his distant kin, having the same grandmother, a septuagenarian crone called in Apache, "The One Who Gibbers Abhorrently in the Leprous Moonlight." As Buck well knew, Granny was not named that for nothing.

It was nigh sundown when he pulled up his maverick at the Rocking Skull Ranch, now operated by the Widder Skull and her two young 'uns, Num and Abner. While Buck tied up his steed at the hitching post, he examined the horizon with his mystic tetrahedron, dredged up from sunken P'u by Roman sponge divers in the year zero, shortly after the second siege of Cacciatore (Uno Maximus Mixupis, or The Big Mixup), disappearing for several years, to surface again in the court of Pharoah Hehahotep IV, and vanishing again for six centuries after the Hyksos' remarkable recovery from supposed extinction. Buck had obtained it by chance through a stroke of luck, having won it in a faro game in Saskatchewan from a mysterious Oriental.

Buck went over the old Indian legends in his mind, legends of certain things lurking beyond the barbed wire fences of the universe . . . the dreaded T'on'to and the abominable Bison Thing, Buffalo B'Hob . . . things that stirred memories of nightmares dreamed by ancient ancestors. Buck was only too well aware of his position as the sole defender of the West against these Red horrors.

He ascended the porch and knocked at the door of the ranchhouse. It was answered by an Indian servant who regarded him with curiously malevolent eyes. This, Buck knew, was Minnie-

by M.M. Moamrath

wahwah, who had faithfully served the Skulls for seven generations or more. Before that she was said to have been in the service of a mysterious stranger calling himself Zane Offwhite. She showed Buck to the sitting room where he waited, and thereafter to the waiting room where he sat for a while chewing his tobacco and spitting into what he assumed was a spittoon. Only after the brass-plated object scuttled off into an opening under the player piano did he apprehend that things were not all they appeared to be.

A creaking board behind him signaled the arrival of a nameless presence. Turning, he saw it was Abner Skull. He recognized him from the old rock carvings on Dead Man's Rock. The man was abnormally tall with a protuberant proboscis and ears resembling nothing more than the outcrop of rimrock at Hanged Man's Canyon. His eyes were cavernous with no living glimmers within. His moustache was more tentacular than hairy and Buck was certain that one of the countless flies milling around that region was snatched from sight by some blurred stringy object.

"Yew thet Eld'rich feller?" asked Skull in a voice that seemed to come from the deepest pits of Dead Man's Mine itself.

"I was sent here by Capt. Gibber to check out the Apache situation," said Buck, his right thumb caressing the hammer of his silver-plated .45.

"Yew shouldn't have oughta cum. We dun't cotton to strangers roun' here. They's things —" He paused, looking over his shoulder. "I've already sed tew much."

"I wonder if the Widder Skull's to home."

"Who?"

"Your mother."

"Oh, yeh. Her. She passed on nigh on two weeks agone. Injuns got 'er. Cut 'er up for jerky and hung 'er on the fence to dry. We got most o' her in the smokehouse now. No sense wastin' none."

The effect of this unexpected revelation unaccountably filled Buck with nameless dread. This sense of foreboding was further increased by Skull's next statement.

"Reckon yew'll hev to best be movin' along. It's gettin' on nightfall and we 'uns got to mosey th' critters on down to New Lemuria."

"New Lemuria? Where's that?"

"Jest south o' New P'u. Goin' south, yew jest make a right turn at the anomaly."

"I never heard of moving cows at night," said Buck.

"Cows? Who said anything about cows?"

Less than an hour later by his clepsydra, Buck and his mount were waiting along the trail to New Lemuria as the Skull boys and several Mexicans moved the Skull herd south. In the leprous moonlight it was hard to tell just what sort of herd was being moved. To the unclad eye it seemed that the lunar beams were filtering down onto the surface of some slick slimy substance. It was necessary to catch a look through his trusty tetrahedron. What he saw nearly sent his mind reeling and gibbering drunkenly over the rimrock of chaos into ghoul haunted regions of madness.

For there, passing below the cliffs, leaving a trail of oozing purple slime in their wake, snorting and puffing like vitreous aqueous humors subjected to the thermal pressures of an aeolopile, was such an accumulation of horrors as had never before been seen upon the terraquaeous globe! *It was a veritable unending stream of suggoths!*

Suggoths!

The very word struck a chord of terror in the cardiovascular organ of any recluse antiquarian with a penchant for the occult. Buck, a master of the occult in his own rite, was only too aware of the meaning of this horror. For the presence of the suggoths, hybrid amorphous creatures whose body in the forepart is that of a cockroach and in the hindpart that of a slug, and once used by the inhabitants of ancient Fuggoth as paperweights, could only signify one thing. . . . Somewhere out beyond the rimrock of primordial chaos, in the vast badlands of the interstellar void, the Fuggothians still existed and were planning to return from their exile beyond the borders of time and space, imposed on them eons ago by S'mucch, High Sheriff of the Aetherial Void.

It was in that instant that Buck realized that only one man stood between the Fuggothians and the destruction of the world as we know it. The Skulls, he realized, were agents of the Fuggothians. As he pondered his unenviable position, the thundering herd of suggoths oozed below him toward their abhorrent destination.

He followed them stealthily on his faithful nag, and it was while the herd sucked their fill at Obed Creek that Ngaio Marsh, a halfbreed Indian, met with the Skull brothers in parley.

It was easy for Buck to see that Ngaio's other half was Fuggothian. It was the way the halfbreed had to ride side-saddle, with his pale slimy slug-like lower quarters dangling to the side. Buck was unable to hear what they were saying, but caught the names of Yuchkkoth the Beclouder, and of Schlusch, Lord of Slime. The halfbreed then removed something from his saddlebags and gave it to Abner Skull. It appeared to be some sort of scroll. Following the foregoing, Ngaio was given payment in firewater and whooped into the hills half astride his pony.

Several hours of hard riding later, Buck watched from the shadowed rimrock above New Lemuria as the suggoths were herded aboard the boxcars of the Wendigo, Dunwent, & Gone, which connected New Lemuria with some nameless region beyond a localized veil of eternal mist into which the narrow-gauge tracks disappeared several miles out of town. Buck knew that if

he was to prevent the range war between the Elderly Gods and the inhabited Southwest, he would have to sneak aboard that train.

After checking the chambers of his twin .45s, he shambled down the cliff and slipped stealthily aboard the caboose just as the train pulled out. A quarter of an hour later a wall of mist loomed before him as the landscape was lost in obscurity. Buck sensed motion, but the familiar clickety-clack of the rails seemed muffled.

Then the black mouth of the tunnel loomed ahead. Buck could remember no hills or mountains in this area. As soon as his eyes became accustomed to the darkness, he perceived numerous twinned sets of glowing orbs, which he took to be eyes. Even as he recalled what the *Negrognomicon* said about things with glowing eyes, he recognized the squat, leprous shapes moving along walkways and niches carved into the tunnel walls, manipulating strange scientifictional machinery that could only have been produced by a super-science far beyond that of man. He knew then that he was in the realm of the dreaded Choo-Choo people, the best trained of the Elderly Gods' minions, who live or otherwise inhabit abandoned railroad tunnels and trestles usually in Tibet.

Then he was no longer in the tunnel (which he now realized was a hyperspacial connection of some sort) and was back in the mist once more. Moments later the train had pulled to a halt, and before he could get his bearings by counting the suns, he heard a noise behind him.

Poking over the edge of the caboose roof was Num Skull.

"Hold 'er rhat thare, boah. Jest unbuckl' yer belt and drap yer hardware. Now climb down offn this caboosie."

Buck perforce obeyed with grim reluctance, promising himself that he would bushwhack Skull and escape at the first opportunity.

He was taken inside the caboose, still without having glimpsed any details of his environs. There he was securely lashed to a pot-belly stove with moistened rawhide. Skull gloated all the while as Minniewahwah tied Buck up. In those dark Indian eyes lurked an unsettling gleam of ancient madness. Also, she was licking her chops.

"Reckon yew bit offn more'n yew kin chaw," drawled Skull, removing a pack of chewing tobacco from his pocket. He held it up to his lips where it was engulfed by the writhing tentacles of his moustache, which began to exude an unpleasant brown fluid that collected on his lower lip before dripping off his chin in large, greasy brown gobbets.

Skull then turned from his captive and sat down at a table with the scroll-like object Ngaio had given him. The Indian woman returned to the end of the car where she began sharpening knives and cutting herbs for supper. Turning his full attention to Skull, Buck watched him unroll the scroll. The end of it was rounded and its surface was strangely coated. Written on it were innumerable pictogryphs, hieroglyphs, inscriptions and other cryptic marks. Buck easily recognized these as variations of the Elder Tongue.

But it was only after Skull had completely unrolled the object to its full length of nine feet that Buck understood that not only was it *written* in the Elder Tongue, but it was an elder tongue itself, probably that of Phyzzwigget, the one-eyed bohemian god who burbles and belches meaningless nothings as he hovers intoxicated at the center of chaos, attended by Durward and Kirby, two tone deaf sycophants with a proclivity for bad jive, by means of which they appease their master, The Howler Beyond the Outside.

But most important, as Buck read the dreaded script over Skull's shoulder, he could see that this was nothing less than a detailed outline whereby the Fuggothians would take over the earth.

He shuddered inwardly.

Fuggothians! The very word made his mind reel with unspeakable loathing. They were native to a planet in the constellation of the Beetle, Alpha Insectus, where they engaged in various nefarious activities and dastardly pursuits under the thirteen blazing suns.

They were remarkably ugly, being part crab, part alligator, part lobster, and a little bit cocker spaniel. Their brains were completely controlled by the dreaded Fungi of Fuggoth, which were at war with streptococcus aurelius and other terrestrial micro-organisms in league with Nerg-Blavvath, Hare of a Thousand Young, for control of earth itself.

Prodded by fear, Buck's thoughts raced ahead of themselves, tripping and sliding through the synapses of his cerebral cortex, and his mind reeled with the terrible knowledge that he, of all men now alive, knew the hideous secret behind the obscure limerick revealed by Bundolo Kreegah in Chapter 67 of the dreaded *Negrognomicon:*

In a cavern under the earth,
Old Nerg-Blavvath gave birth
To a dog and a cat,
A cow and a bat,
And all without aid of a nurse.

As he watched Minniewahwah glancing over her shoulder, licking her chops while chopping herbs and sharpening knives, Buck wondered whether he would ever escape to pass word to Capt. Gibber. But at that moment, the moving train lurched to a halt, and the mist cleared. Buck counted thirteen suns shining through the window.

"Holy hot tamales," he blasphemed involuntarily. If only he could free himself! But it was too late, for the crone was coming at him with the knife.

"Heh, I'll jest leave yew tew alone," drawled Skull. "I know yew have privat biznuz to dee-scus." He exited. Outside, Buck could hear the suggoths being unloaded. Undoubtedly the Skulls had been raising them on earth under an agreement with the Fuggothians to exempt the ranch and its inhabitants from the general massacre which would ensue when earth was invaded.

He knew it was curtains for him, but in the last moment before she plunged her knife down, Minniewahwah slipped in a puddle of tobacco juice and fell against the stove, her knife accidentally slicing Buck's bonds. Recovering his twin six-shooters, he exited via the forward door, climbing atop the boxcars to creep from car to car toward the locomotive.

Only one minion stood guard there, a slouching, lazy-looking Choo-Choo, surely an atypical example of the species. With a swipe of his pearl handled pistol, Buck laid him low and stuffed him into the fire grate. He then released the brake, turned up the steam, and threw the engine in reverse.

The consternation among the Fuggothians was immense. The spooked suggoths panicked and slithered off in all directions, crashing through fences and outbuildings, and as the train picked up speed, Buck picked off his confused assailants with neatly placed slugs from his .45s.

Then the train was enveloped in the weird mist, and once more the huge dark shape of the tunnel engulfed him. From somewhere came a rumble of thunder, and soon the tunnel mouth behind him was illuminated by weird hellish lightning flashes, probably the result of the train's warping the space-time continuum.

And in the darkness of the hyperspacial tunnel, he could see the glowing eyes of the Choo-Choos glaring with surprise, and he watched them frantically throwing the switches of their weird Gernsbackian devices.

He watched with horror as some of them leapt aboard the train from the tunnel walls.

Grimly, he drew his guns and blazed away with both barrels as they came at him. He watched with satisfaction as pair after pair of glowing eyes winked out, but they kept coming. Already they were scuttling over the coal car even as the train burst free of the tunnel.

Amazingly, it was raining, and bull-whips of lightning flailed the rumps of black thunderheads stampeding across the sky.

Apparently the space warp caused by the reversed train had been more powerful than he realized. He thought he saw the eyes of the Choo-Choos exude fearful gleams as they looked about them, but then his guns ran out of bullets and he prepared to be overwhelmed by the vile alien horrors.

Just then, when he had already consigned his spirit to that big tally book in the sky, angry lightning forked down from the heavens and blasted the Choo-Choos to smithereens. Then he smiled grimly, for he remembered the hitherto obscure reference of Kreegah to the Choo-Choos, ". . . it is said that the Choo-Choos are good conductors . . ."

But he was not yet safe. For there, whooping along the tops of the boxcars was Minniewahwah, brandishing a tomahawk.

Just then, the crone's moccasins fortuitously slipped on the rain slick boxcar roof. And she fell, impaled on her weapon.

As Buck leaned over her, he saw she was trying to croak a message, and it was then he recognized something familiar in that batrachian visage.

"Doesn't Minniewahwah mean 'The One Who Gibbers Abhorrently in the Leprous Moonlight'?" he asked.

"Yes, my little buckeroo," croaked the crone. "It is I, your Granny. And Ngaio was your half-brother."

"Don't try to talk, Granny," said Buck, a tear welling in his eye.

"Must — must talk," she wheezed, "must tell you — tell you — couplet — dreaded couplet —" And then she summoned her waning strength and in a

burst of lucidity gibbered abhorrently in the leprous moonlight

"That is not led which eternally follows.
And if you're in Capistrano
look out for the swallows."

With that, she expired.

By sunup, Buck was back at New Lemuria, where his cayuse was waiting. He was surprised to find Old Paint had somehow thrown a shoe from his left middle tentacle, but fortunately there was a blacksmith in town.

Oh, well, he thought, eying the rising sun, the day is shot anyhow.

Kissing his cayuse tenderly on the mandibles, he led it away to the smithy. "Well, you know what they say," he told Old Paint. "If you can't ride off into the sunset, don't ride off at all."

BEHIND THE MUSIC

by Craig Shaw Gardner

illustrated by P.D. O'Main

They called him Lonesome George, but he didn't care. He'd gone West to be alone, after it hadn't worked out with the school marm. And he had in his possession the three things that every cowboy needs — his trusty horse, his trusty six-gun, and his trusty guitar.

Now those of you who don't truly know the West may ask a question here. The need of a trusty horse is obvious, both as a means of transportation, and as a boon companion, far less fickle than your average school marm. The need of a trusty gun is equally clear, for the West in those days was a Wild place, full of Outlaws who might shoot you before you said hello, and Indians who might not look kindly on your walking across their property, not to mention wild beasts who might tear the gunless limb from limb. But a guitar? Why would a Cowboy need a trusty guitar?

Well, I'm here to tell you why a guitar was the most useful instrument of all.

Now, on the day when this all began, Lonesome George should have been happy. The day, while hot, was not unbearably so, and while George and his horse Faithful were traversing a particularly dry corner of the West, George had a full canteen and a map showing a watering hole at not too great a distance.

But George was at odds with himself. He had just finished working a cattle drive, and then to top it off had won at poker in a final farewell game, so his saddlebags were full of folding money. One would think this would make him happier still. But the job was done, and George had departed the stockyards in

Kansas City with no clear plans for his future, just the vague notion of riding someplace interesting. San Francisco, maybe. Or the wild border towns of Mexico. Or the unexplored regions of Oregon territory. Like I said, his notions were vague, but they all pointed in one direction.

So he had headed even farther West, into this dry, dusty expanse filled with not much more than sagebrush and stones. And he had to admit, he might have entered a part of the West that was even too lonesome for him. For George hadn't seen another human being for the better part of a week. Heck, he hadn't seen a jackrabbit or a prairie dog for the last couple days. And now that he thought of it, the sky above them for the last few hours had been completely empty of birds.

Faithful whinnied as he trotted ahead, as if even the horse sensed something was amiss.

Maybe, George reflected, it would be a good idea to turn back. But the watering hole wasn't that far ahead. Besides, he was heading West. It was just a little too quiet here. That was all.

No critters. No birds. Not even a vulture. Nothing.

George checked his gear. He had a loaded six shooter at his belt, a Winchester strapped to his saddle, food and water enough for three days, and of course the last thing he has won at the poker game when Easy Ed had come up short of cash — that durned guitar. Well, George thought, he had plenty to eat, ample means of protection, and he supposed he could even entertain himself by strumming a tune or two. He turned away from his inventory to look at the trail ahead.

The cowboy's mouth fell open in astonishment.

He saw a man standing in their path, maybe a hundred yards away. Where had the stranger come from? George could see no cover the man could have stepped from, nor any means of transportation that might have brought him here, no horses, no buggies, no caves or convenient trees, not even a large cactus, nothing for as far as he could see. Yet here was somebody straight ahead of them where a moment before there had been nothing at all.

Faithful snorted in apprehension.

The figure ahead raised his right hand in greeting. The stranger appeared to be an Indian, wrapped in tribal blankets despite the heat. As George grew closer, he noted that the man also appeared to be very old, his body hunched forward, his face a weathered map of lines and wrinkles.

George may have been a loner, but he was polite. He tipped his hat as he approached.

"Welcome, traveler!" the Indian intoned in a voice as deep as the nearby canyons. "Out of all the others, it is you to whom I must speak."

"Others?" George frowned. "What do you mean, old man? Am I not the first to ride through here?"

The elder Indian nodded sagely. "There were three before you this very day. But you are the first I have greeted."

And why would that be? But the old Indian answered George before he even had a chance to frame the question.

"It is true. I have not warned the others. But you are different. After all, you have a guitar."

George thought he might take exception to that — seeing as how the guitar had come to him by accident. But how could he argue with something he did not understand?

"Beg pardon?" George asked instead.

At that, the ancient Indian's eyes, mere slits in his weathered, wrinkle-heavy countenance, opened ever so slightly, as if even the wisest of the wise might be surprised. "But you do not realize the danger!"

"Danger?" George echoed, his hand automatically reaching for the gun on his belt. "What danger?"

"Have you looked at the rocks recently?" was the old man's reply.

Rocks? Besides the dirt and the sagebrush, he had seen nothing but rocks these last few hours. George spotted a pile of them immediately behind the old man. Funny. He hadn't noticed any piles of rocks before. But then, he hadn't seen the old Indian either. The prairie sun must be playing tricks on him.

The old man nodded sagely. George began to suspect the stranger could nod in no other way.

"The rocks. It is not what you see. It is what you do not see." The Indian pointed quite abruptly at a point past George's shoulder.

"Over there!" the old man exclaimed.

George spun his trusty horse, ready for any danger. But all he saw was the same quiet, endless prairie.

He urged Faithful back towards the Indian.

"But there's nothing —" He stopped abruptly as he saw that the pile of rocks just past the old man had tripled in size, and leaned in such a way that the stones — some of them quite large — threatened to fall upon the senior at any moment.

"Exactly!" the elder added with the wisest of smiles.

George scratched the mop of hair beneath his ten gallon hat. "So you're telling me that if you don't look out, the rocks will sneak up on you?"

"That is only the beginning of the terrible truth." George realized the old man no longer turned away from the looming mound. "You do not wish to witness what would happen if these rocks should have their way."

"Then they're just waiting there to — crush you?" the cowboy asked.

He was answered by another wise nod. "Yes, that, and more. For these rocks are man-eaters."

Even Faithful took a step away at that.

"Man-eaters?"

"Man, horse, supplies, and anything else that gets in their way," the elder explained.

Now, a statement like this challenged even George's good nature. "If this is true, old man," he demanded, "then why aren't we running for our lives?"

"As I have said, the rocks only attack when you are not looking. But when they strike, they are faster than sight, quieter than the breeze, as deadly as your darkest dream. Allow me to demonstrate."

He had pulled an entire roasted rabbit on a spit from somewhere within his blanket-covered form. He took a few quick steps away from the looming pile, then tossed the rabbit to a spot just short of the rocks.

"Look away for a minute."

George did as he was instructed. His horse started as they heard a terrible grinding noise. George spun about to see the pile of rocks more or less unchanged. But the rabbit was gone.

Did he see that the slightest dark spot in the sand where the carcass had lain? And was it his imagination, or did the pile of rocks appear a little plumper? George thought again about the grinding noise. It was not a sound he wished to hear again.

"You see the truth in my words," the elder intoned.

Lonesome George whistled. "I see the truth in getting ourselves the heck out of here!"

But the wise man didn't budge. "It would do no good. Once the rocks have marked you, they will follow you forever."

George looked around. Another pile of rocks had appeared behind the old man's feet. And yet another had begun to grow just to the left of George's horse.

The cowboy stared at this newest pile. The rocks didn't move as he watched. They just sat there as still as stone. He would have imagined they had been there forever.

George blinked. The pile looked twice as tall as before. It seemed there was no escape. He turned to the Indian. "Why are you telling me this? So I can prepare to die?"

The ancient wise one shook his head at last.

"I am in no danger, for I can sing!"

With that the old man launched into a long string of strange syllables, far beyond George's understanding. Something like: "Winnie-na na-noo nooo-wanna-gonna shoulda-coulda na-no-ninnie-ninnie-hey!" Or words to that effect.

A great wind sprung up from nowhere. George had to shield his eyes from the blowing dust.

The pile of rocks was gone as well. All the piles were gone. Aside from the occasional stone left here and there in the dirt, the entire vista was rock-free.

Lonesome George was impressed.

"The rocks are no match for the pure of voice," the elder affirmed.

"But begging your pardon," added

George, who was still a bit shaken, "I don't know if I'm up to all that mystic chanting."

"Ah, but you have your own version of the remedy. For you can sing. And play your guitar. It is the same."

"Sing?" George asked. "And play?"

"Yes. Should you do so with spirit, you will vanquish the rocks forever."

George looked doubtfully at the guitar slung to the back of his saddle. "That's it? Nothing else?"

The Indian thought for a moment. "Perhaps it will be even better if you yodel."

George might have thought he deserved more explanation, but the wise elder shook his head and pointed further West.

"Go now and find the others. You are their only hope." He paused in that way wise men had, only to add for dramatic effect, "The rocks are hungry."

George still thought there might be time for a question or two, but the old man folded his arms before him as he continued to speak.

"I am old and know much. But my part in this story is done."

Then, in the way of Mystic Spirit Guides everywhere, and accompanied by the usual great wind, he up and disappeared.

Faithful snorted with trepidation.

The cowboy patted his horse's neck. "Come on now, old boy. It's gonna be all right."

George wished he really felt those words. What else could he do? He and his horse rode West to fulfill their destiny.

He saw another man on horseback riding in his direction. The newcomer's clothes were the color of the dust, and the frown on his face seemed like a permanent part of his outfit.

"Freeze, stranger!" the newcomer greeted George. He glared suspiciously as George politely tipped his hat.

"I'm the County Marshall. People have been disappearing hereabouts under mysterious circumstances." The lawman tugged at his mustache in a purposeful fashion. "You wouldn't know anything about that, now would you?"

George thought about a possible answer to give the lawman. And immediately rejected any and all response. For George knew that there are certain people who you can tell about man-eating rocks. And then there are no-nonsense folks like the Marshall. Start talking about something foolish like that, and the lawman might shoot you just to be on the safe side.

"I notice you have a guitar," the Marshall said to break the silence.

George nodded. "I won it in a poker game."

"So they all say." The Marshall's frown grew deeper still.

George frowned back. He was beginning to dislike the lawman's attitude. "Is there a problem?"

"I never thought playing the guitar was particularly manly." The lawman snorted derisively, then stared into the distance. "Nowhere near as manly as hunting through the wilderness for the disappeared."

George frowned as he noticed a pile of rocks just past the Marshall and his horse.

"Why don't we ride as we talk?" George suggested. "I've heard, out in the wild, it's best not to stay in one place."

"So you say," the Marshall did not quite agree. "If you don't mind, why don't you ride ahead?"

They rode for a few minutes. Neither man spoke. Until George saw the rocks further on.

"Whoa!" George exclaimed, reigning in his horse. "What's this?"

Directly in front of them was a hole in the ground, surrounded by piles of rocks. Lonesome George feared the worst.

But George realized that the silence of this place was interrupted by digging noises, punctuated by the occasional whistle and the more than occasional cough.

The Marshall nodded towards the hole. "That would be Toothless Ned."

An aged but not-particularly wise head popped up from the hole. "How do, Marshall? Lookin' to stake a claim?"

"Nope, Ned," the lawman replied. "I've got another job to do. You see anything funny hereabouts?"

"Tarnation! Nothin' funny at all. Just me and the rocks!"

But couldn't they see? They were surrounded by rocks — surrounded by danger! Perhaps George would have to do some explaining after all.

"Before I ran into you, Marshall," George began, "I met this old Indian—"

George's explanation was interrupted by an astonishingly lengthy and unhealthy sounding coughing fit on the part of the prospector.

"Land o' Goshen!" Ned exclaimed when he was finally able to draw breath again. "Pardon me while I light up a smoke and clear my lungs."

George watched as the prospector pulled a hand-rolled cigarette from his vest. He realized the Marshall was watching Ned as well. During their conversation, the three of them had been totally focused on each other.

None of them had been paying any attention to the rocks.

George whipped his head about to take in the situation. As he feared, each of the three now had a new pile of rocks nearby, with each pile tall enough to crush the nearest human. But the largest pile loomed right above Ned.

"Watch out!" he called, reaching quickly for his guitar.

"No sudden moves now!" The Marshall looked ready to go for his gun.

"It's not me. It's the rocks!" He tried to remember the simple chords he'd learned as a boy.

"What rocks?" The lawman once again reached for his pistol. "You start talkin' crazy and I'll shoot you!"

But even the Marshall paused as he saw the great pile of stone looming above him. "What the—"

"Guns are no good now! We only have one hope." George strummed quickly on his guitar, keeping one eye on the pile teetering over his ten gallon hat. "Sing for all you're worth!"

"By thunder! Sing?" Ned coughed. "I can barely breathe!"

Off the top of his head, George sang a couplet about riding on the trail watching for a coyote's tail, or something of the sort.

The rocks seemed to give George a little room.

The Marshall, almost lost under the shadow of a great pile of stone, quickly brought forth some of his own snatches of melody, something about bringing in the sheaves with Sweet Betsy from Pike. But George heard nothing from the prospector.

"There's only one way out!" he encouraged as he continued to strum. "Sing, Ned, sing!"

But all he heard from the hole was another wracking cough.

He glanced about. The rocks were piling up on his other side. George quickly sang about the mountains high in the clear blue sky. The Marshall sang a few new snatches of his own. This time, Betsy seemed to be bringing in the sheaves herself.

"Ned!" George sang.

But all he heard in reply was that cough, followed by that terrible grinding noise. He looked back to see the hole that once held the prospector was now filled with a pile of stones.

Ned was gone. George realized there was more than one way tobacco could kill you.

But, as he looked about, he saw that the other rocks had retreated! The piles were still there, but they had somehow repositioned themselves a few feet away.

"We've got to get Ned out of there!" the Marshall cried.

It was George's turn to shake his head. "It wouldn't do any good. Once the rocks have their way with a fella, there's nothing left."

"The rocks?" the lawman asked.

"Man-eaters," George confirmed.

The shock on the Marshall's face seemed to be giving way to his usual skeptical expression. "And they didn't eat us because?"

"They were pushed back by the power of song."

The Marshall glanced around. "They didn't push very far. If you don't come up with a better explanation —"

But the lawman's threat was interrupted by the arrival of a noisy buckboard. George looked away from the rocks long enough to see the wagon was driven by a young and not unattractive woman, dressed all in cowgirl white!

"Something's happened to Ned!" she said as she jumped from the wagon.

The Marshall pointed at the stone-filled pit. "He's under there."

"The rocks got him," George added.

The young woman nodded. "I haven't liked the look of these rocks for days."

George took an instant liking to this newcomer. He tipped his hat and introduced himself. She smiled prettily in return, saying, "You can call me Dale."

George liked that even more. Unlike — say — Mary Sue or Noreen, Dale was a real Western name!

"Now Dale, I've told you you shouldn't be out here," the Marshall began.

The young woman glared back at the lawman, her hands on her hips. "What else could I do? I don't have the talents for a saloon gal, and school marming don't suit my disposition, so I took up exploring."

Exploring? thought Lonesome George. Not only did this woman have a Western name, she had a Western spirit!

The Marshall snorted. "Can you imagine a woman —" But then he hesitated. "Aren't the rocks getting closer?"

George nodded. "They sneak up on you when you're not looking."

"But they're all around us! We can't be looking everywhere!" The lawman appeared to be losing his ice cool demeanor.

"This guitar has scared them off before." George strummed a powerful chord. "Let's see what happens when we all work together."

So George once again started in to sing. This time, it was June and spoon on the honeymoon. And gal and pal in the old corral. The tunes just kept flowing out. With Dale around, he was downright inspired!

The Marshall hummed in harmony, adding the occasional "get along little dogie" or some such whenever appropriate.

The rocks didn't attack. In fact, the piles seemed to have retreated a bit.

"We're drivin' 'em back!" the Marshall exclaimed. "But they won't go away!"

What else could they do? George thought of the old wise man's words.

"I just wish I knew how to yodel!" George exclaimed.

"Is that all?" Dale asked with a grin.

She opened her mouth wide, and her voice trilled magnificently, whooping and hollering, her yodel echoing across the plains. George grinned. With a name like Dale, he should have expected no less!

They were surrounded again by a great wind. George had to close his eyes for an instant against the dust. But when he opened them, the rocks were gone. There wasn't a loose stone between here and the horizon!

"Whoohoo!" the Marshall declared. "That did it!" He turned back to Lonesome George. "Maybe playing a guitar is manly after all."

But George was otherwise occupied. He looked deep into Dale's eyes as he complemented her on her yodel. She, in turn, marveled at the sensitivity of George's lyrics counterpointed only by the robustness of his tunes. It was obvious to anyone, even the Marshall, that Lonesome George was destined to be lonesome no more.

Even Faithful whinnied in contentment.

"Well," the Marshall added, "now that we've solved the mystery of the disappeared, I suppose I'll go back to foiling bank robberies, shooting rustlers, and more of the usual. What about you folks?"

Dale looked at George. George looked at Dale.

George said, "Why, we are headed West."

And so they were, to show cowboys and cowgirls everywhere that while they needed their trusty guns and trusty horses, they should never, ever forget a well-sung yodel and a well-tuned guitar.

And with that, George and Dale climbed up on the buckboard (with Faithful tied behind) and began that long ride to their Destiny, and Happy Trails.

GHOSTLY LIMERICK

A ghost haunts a grove of mesquite:
A lady so slim and petuite
    She moves with the breeze
    Among the green treeze
And leaves not a print of her fuite.
— **Ed Ward**

by **Craig Shaw Gardner**

NEW GODS FOR OLD
beginning an exciting new serial
by P. D. "Tequila-Cured" Cacek
illustrated by Keith Minnion

Everything about the barren, wind-blasted, desiccated landscape of which he had — so innocently — placed himself, of which — for better (HAH!) or worse (likely) — he was now a part, was wrong.

Terribly, unexpectedly *wrong!*

Even the sun, which had been unquestionably and scientifically constant in the East, now showed signs of deviance. For it still hung, as it had for the last few hours — pendulous and swollen like an overripe carbuncle about to burst — within a mere two-fingers span above a craggy, purple-hued, featureless horizon. Of course, he was only estimating the distance being thus, for if he were to actually extend his arm to its full length and crook both his index and middle fingers to take an accurate measure . . . it would undoubtedly incurred more dubious stares from both his fellow passengers and the coach driver.

It'd been obvious from the very first moment his initial tantrum upon the sagging and weathered steps of what *The West* considered a train station — an honest reaction, he thought, considering his expectations of what a *"Staged coach"* was and the utter devastating reality it turned out to be — that *Westerners* simply did not know how to react to a gentleman who had been literally and figuratively steeped in *Eastern* sensibilities.

The stares had been cold and rat-like, dripping with ill-concealed contempt and callous disregard . . . and this had been from the four "Mail-order Brides" who were to be his traveling companions. The mindless gapes he received from the coach-driver and various other inconsequential bystanders who had gathered to watch his anguish were just too demeaning to recall.

And he would have, if things had been different, pulled himself from the drab, ecru-tinted dust and immediately bought a return ticket — a single, one-way — back to the Eldritch-haunted glades and humid air of his beloved *East.*

But things were not different and he, Atticus Fritzwaller Plughe, had only brought this devastation upon himself.

Innocently, of course.

"An innocent lamb led to the slaughter by what seemed to be the truest of friends," he whispered, sorrowfully, to himself . . . and felt the *western* wind throw it back in his face.

Hah hah, it seemed to hiss as it spiraled toward the never-setting sun. *More fool you, Atticus Fritzwaller Plughe. Hah, hah!*

True, so true. Fool had he been to listen to what he now believed to be nothing more than vicious malevolence on the part of one he thought a friend. Øystein Zacharias Smith, whose imperfect sense of humor (or guile) had caused him to send Atticus the 1851 Indiana newspaper clipping of one John Soule.

"Go West Young Man" indeed!

And if *The West* had truly been as a beckoning light amid the all-consuming waves of Eastern expansion, than why — *Atticus asked for the millionth time, again to himself* — had not his friend accompanied him?

More over, why hadn't his venerated family tried to stop him when he laid his plan before them one dark and stormy mid-summer's eve three months prior? It had been a ludicrous idea at best . . . a young and foolish man's fancy . . . but his family, especially his father —

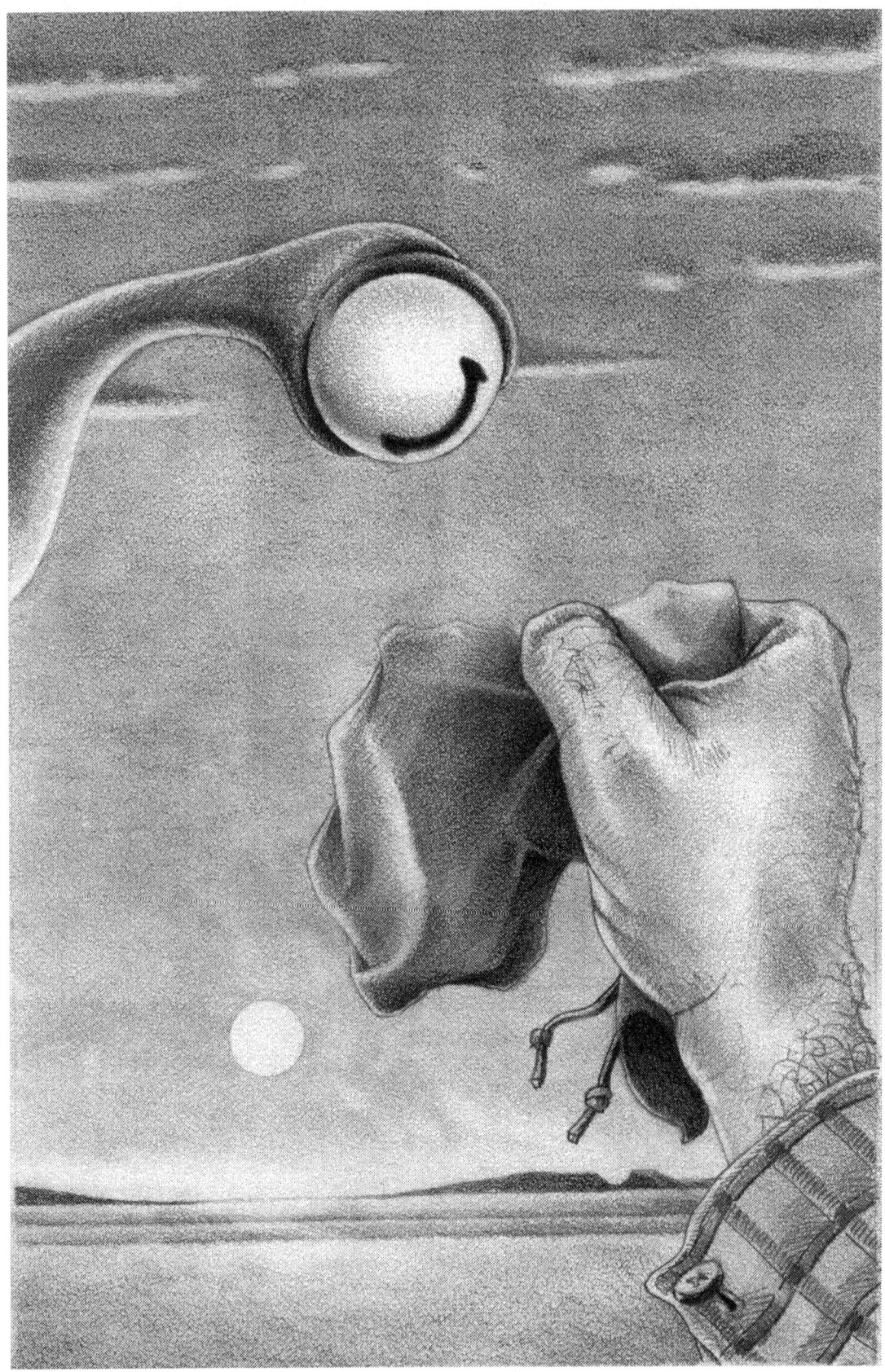

the current overseeing patriarch, had adhered to the thought as if it suddenly sprouted tentacles which had wrapped themselves around the great man's hydrocephalic body.

"Yes, Father," Atticus had said, with so much assuredness it made his bones ache, *"then if The West is as amenable to change as Mr. Soule would have us believe, and we all know the high standards of faithfulness and veracity to which newspapermen adhere, then that far unseen land of vast vistas, endless possibilities and 'godless heathens' could not be better suited to the needs and multi-membered reach of our Great and Terrifying Lords. For you must admit, Father, that far too many eyes on this side of the globe have witnessed and written about the glorious miracles and ventures of our Eldritch masters."*

And his father, sitting tucked into one corner of the crimson-velvet méridenne lounge, resplendent in chartreuse brocade and tassels, and holding a crystalline snifter betwixt both hands while blue-white smoke curled lazily upward from the well-used and ash-trayed meerschaum pipe, nodded in agreement.

Atticus had been so filled with righteous pride that he had, quite literally, popped a button from his vest. The button, gold in color and stamped with the visage of a roaring lion, flew across the room and, due to the capricious whim of whichever Old One happened to be watching at that moment, struck and immediately killed the aged, incontinent and continually molting parrot his mother kept solely to annoy the household staff.

"My dearest progeny," his father had said, "you have always been my particular favorite among those of my children which lived past infancy. Do you wish to know why?"

"Oh, yes, Father," Atticus had said, a grave and inquiring look fixed upon his slightly asymmetrical features. "Do tell."

And his father did.

"It is because you, among all your remaining siblings, have shown that most rare of qualities: genuine initiative. While your siblings are content to sprawl in the secure and familiar stygian depths of adequacy, you, my dearest Atticus, have always strived to see what is beyond the horizon even if there is nothing save a hellish drop to dismemberment and oblivion."

His father then lifted the snifter in a two-handed salute. "I am so very proud of you, dearest son."

Another button on Atticus's vest trembled in preparation of flight, but stalled when his father removed his proboscis from the snifter after taking a healthy slurp and pointed it in Atticus's general direction.

"And I will give you my permission to venture forth on this most noble venture . . . on one condition."

Atticus's pride-swollen chest deflated slightly. "Yes, Father?"

"I desire that your elder brother, Plecostomus, accompany you."

Atticus's chest continued to deflate until it was more concave than convex. "But, Father," Atticus said with all due respect. "With all due respect, and as much as I admire and hold my elder sibling in the utmost veneration, Plecostomus is nothing more than a supercilious and highly apathetic slug."

"That is, alas, all too true," his father said desolately, because it was, after all, the truth. "But so superlative is the magnitude of your endeavor, that I daresay even an indolent slug like your brother may benefit from the mere proximity of it.

"Yes, dear Atticus, go West, young man and establish the foothold of a new dynasty among the as yet untapped resources and psyches of the unsuspecting and unwashed . . . but don't forget your brother, that's a good lad."

Nodding to one parent, but hoping to find clemency from another, Atticus had turned from his father to his mother . . . only to find her, the flowing hem of her gown daintily tucked in around her, squatting next to the excrement-decorated brass perch and, with great refinement, picking clean the bones of her recently-departed pet.

She smiled when their eyes met and a pin-feather, caught betwixt her Equus Caballus-like front teeth, quivered.

"Mind your father, dear," she said, her sweet voice ringing like that of a funeral knell as she snapped the parrot's wishbone in preparation of sucking out the marrow. "And remember always how proud I am of you at this moment."

How proud of him would she be now, Atticus wondered as he stared at the unmoving *Western* sun. He had been wrong to make the journey and so terribly wrong with his preconceived presumption about *The West.*

The "vast vistas" he had visualized as wilder versions of well maintained city parks through which a myriad of exotic creatures slithered were endless panoramas consisting of red rock and bone-white sand that supported only the most rudimentary — and surprisingly sharp — vegetation. And whatever "endless possibilities" there may have been when *The West's* maidenhood was first breached, now seemed overflowing with unkempt and blank-eyed red men: Those Easterners who hadn't heeded the warnings of knowledgeable clothiers and gone to seek fame and or fortune without benefit of oversized headgear and thus had permanently and forever changed their once pristine pallor to opulent vermillion.

Atticus, in his innocent excitement, had even been wrong about *The West* being filled with "godless heathens" . . . and he vowed, should he be able to return, to write Newspaperman Soule a scathing rebuttal. For *The West* did have a god, a very powerful and prolific one.

A god that had so little fear of Atticus and the divine race of Elders whom he served, that it presented itself to him within moments of his dusting the last of his tantrum from his trousers and demanding that a *proper* Coach and Four, befitting his exalted rank and supremacy, be procured immediately.

The god had bided its time while the Mail-order brides twittered behind lace handkerchiefs and the *Staged coach driver* shot Atticus another dubious gape.

"Wha'cho tal'king 'bout, bouy?"

And perhaps *The Western* god had even laughed at that moment, a silent, smirking laugh that was lost in the soft jangle of harness chains as the horses shifted their massive weight. Perhaps so — for Atticus now knew how devious this *New God of The West* was. But at that place and time, however, he was still innocent . . . still, may the Old Ones forgive him, malleable.

"I'm talking about—" Atticus said once he'd deciphered the man's words. "—obtaining a conveyance suitable for me, and my luggage, in which to continue the passage *Westward.*"

There were more twitters from the *Staged coach's* murky interior, more shifting of horseflesh and, of course, another round of dubious stares.

"Thisen 'eres t'onliness way west, yung feller. Train dun't go n'further'n this point'n yer ticket says yer gwain'n amite b'yond."

Atticus hoped that his open-mouthed gape, as he stared up at the driver, had a certain dubious quality to it. Head aching and ears tingling at the mangled utterances, Atticus had lifted himself to his full 5'7" (with the help of extenders cleverly hidden in the soles of his special-order boots) height and taken one step forward when the driver reached into the pocket of his greasy, perspiration-stained, permanently faded calico shirt and pulled out what looked like a gnarled and twisted, fire-blackened bone.

Having seen such things before, usually at the supper table for his mother was nothing if not a fine gourmet chef,

Atticus continued his descent down the weather-worn stairs as the driver placed the *bone* betwixt his remaining two back molars and gnawed off a small portion.

The transformation was instantaneous.

First the man's face imploded as though he'd just bitten into a green lemon, causing the tears that had formed in his eyes to squirt into the dry air as if ejected from a fire-hose. Body shaking, booted feet obliviously drumming against the wooded footboard, Atticus watched with a mix of horror and fascination as the hand which held the *bone* rose skyward.

It was as pure an act of piety as Atticus had ever seen. But if that in itself hadn't been enough to convince him that he was indeed in the presence of a divine being, the change which came over the *Staged coach* driver was more than enough evidence he needed.

With tears of fervor still rolling down the furrows in his face, the driver wiped his nose on the sleeve of his shirt — the sleeve covering the arm, the hand of which still held the *bone-like* deity — and fixed a fore-shortened stare toward the far horizon.

"Well, young sir," the man said, his speech and mannerism so profoundly altered that those passersby who had loitered during their previous conversation feigned boredom and scurried slowly away. "I understand your qualms about this vehicle, but, as I have afore mentioned, this *is* the only means of transport to the destination indicated on your ticket. In another five years time, perhaps, there may well be rails laid to all points west . . . for now, however and with my deepest apologies to your unquestionably impressive upbringing, you must travel with me if you wish to go farther.

"Utterstand?"

Atticus nodded, his eyes never leaving the dark, twisted object in the man's hand.

"Wha?" the driver said, obviously reverting back to the coarse, loutish identity as so not to frighten his feminine passengers whose twitterings had taken on a raucous quality.

"That," Atticus replied, indication which *that* he was referring to with a slightly trembling digit. "What is that . . . called?"

The man's eyes slowly turned toward the gnarled object — the left eye reaching its destination a few seconds before the right. "This? Hail bouy, this'ens apluga t'baccy. Wanna chaw?"

Wannachaw? Apluga? T'baccy? Atticus had never heard of such an expressive name . . . if name it was, but bowed his head and nodded solemnly. His parents had taught him to show the proper respect of all things — up until the moment the thing could be killed, eaten or otherwise incapacitated.

"Wannachaw Apluga T'baccy," he repeated —

— and was stunned into near collapse when a small fragment of *Wannachaw Apluga T'baccy* suddenly appeared on the dusty wooden step next to his right foot. There were teeth marks present and one end, the one closest to his foot, glistened wetly with what, Atticus could only surmise, was mahogany-brown blood. Good — a god that bled was a god that could be subdued.

Trembling from head to toe — unquestionably from fatigue — Atticus braced himself for whatever might happen, and bent down to retrieve the portion of deity.

Nothing happened.

Nothing whatsoever.

There was absolutely *no* sensation: no bone-crushing tremor, no vision of a world beaten into submission, not even the whisper of an unearthly voice that could overtake and fill all those who heard it with awe and dread. There was . . . nothing . . . nothing but the very ordinary feel of it against his fingers.

Atticus looked up, puzzled, and saw the man's eyes roll skyward. "Stickit inta yer gob, bouy . . . ain't gonna do ya anny good jist holtin' it."

It took a moment, but Atticus's superior mental powers finally translated the directions and placed the fragment — carefully — into his mouth.

"Now, jist bite down an' git ready t'meet para dice."

Atticus bit down.

And thought he didn't see a pair of dice, the world as he knew it vanish beneath a gut-wrenching, mind-exploding rush of impressions that literally dropped him to his knees. The last thing he remembered seeing, just before oblivion swept over him, was the bonneted heads of the four Mail-Order Brides as they lifted him bodily into the *Staged coach.*

When reality returned, sometime later, Atticus found himself hanging from one of the coach's "windows" decorating the drab landscape with bile as the pinched-faced spinsters, looking to better their lots in their declining years, hung onto his coattails.

It'd been a miserable experience, made more so because Atticus had been sure he'd heard *Apluga T'baccy* (for he had learned from listening to the "Brides to Be" that *Wannachaw* seemed to be the formal expression of solemn ratification) the insidious god of *The West* sniggering with each mile that brought them closer to this . . . their final destination.

"Summin' t'matter, bouy?"

Atticus blinked his eyes at *The Western* sun and withdrew the solid gold chronograph from his waistcoat pocket as he turned around.

"The sun's wrong," he told the coach driver, holding the watch up as proof. "It should have set three hours ago."

The man's chuckle had a demeaning edge that he had not tried to conceal.

"Mebbe in t'east, bouy," the man said. "Yer in t'west now . . . bestta git used tit."

The "Ladies" in the coach twittered and Atticus felt the ire rush to his cheeks. If it hadn't been for the close proximity of the fragment of *Apluga T'baccy* (*Wannachaw!*) in the driver's hand — for Atticus had deduced throughout the long and nauseating trip that so great and devious was *Apluga T'baccy* that only a small portion of itself was needed to keep control of its widely scattered supplicants — he would have called upon the Old Ones and had the man reduced to a pile of ash.

If the Old Ones had been closer, that is . . . and he could be sure this *Western* deity wouldn't have proven too much for Them.

It was at that moment, when the first cancerous doubt of divine supremacy had crept into Atticus soul, that he realized if he was to succeed in his quest he needed to learn the full potency of *Apluga T'baccy* . . . and if he could use it to his — and the Old One's, of course — advantage.

Wannachaw!

Replacing the watch into his pocket as twilight finally settled upon *The West,* Atticus bowed his head and lifted one hand in supplication.

"*Apluga T'baccy,*" he said as fervently as the bile rising in his throat would allow . . . and was startled into momentary silence when a wet *glob* of the god's dark blood landed an inch from the front of his boots.

Atticus stumbled backwards; the hand he'd lifted now clenched to the front of his chest, and looked up in reasonable horror. The *Staged coach* driver was smirking at him, a thin line of mahogany-colored drool sliding down his stubble-bedecked chin. So shocked was Atticus in fact, that he — again momentarily — forgot to feign meekness.

"How *dare* you!" he ejaculated.

And the driver's lips twitched as if he were about to apologize for his actions as well as living in such an unfathomably prosaic and retrogressive society which allow such things . . . right before spitting another globule of *Apluga*

T'baccy's blood onto the platform on which Atticus stood.

Red of face and seething with moral outrage, Atticus was about to begin gibbering incoherently when the driver took notice and batted the air with his hands.

"Simmer down," the man said, "simmer down . . . ah missed ya by least a mile."

Collecting himself, Atticus carefully walked around the divine blood that was even now seeping into the worn planks. "Be that as it may," he said, "there was no reason for such a vulgar display to my simple request."

"Simple r'quest?" the driver chortled. "Son, ah seen m'share o'younin's like ya who think they're upta apluga . . . but ya 'were th'first t'spend mosta th' trip a-hangin' out t'winder. Ain't no way ah'm a-gonna giveya achaw if all yah're gonna do is feed it back t'the snakes."

All Atticus could decipher from that was the negative.

"But I . . ." It was hard, but Atticus knew what had to be done and he did it. He begged. "I . . . need *Apluga T'baccy.*"

Atticus was surprised to see a softening around the man's rat-like eyes. "Caught'cha this soon, huh? Wall . . . ah think there's some less prime stuff in town 'might suit yore innards better'n this."

And he teased Atticus by lifting the divine fragment and waving it at him. *Just wait, you gibbonous fool. The moment I subdue and bend your* Western *god to my . . . to the Old One's will, you'll see what pain and degradation truly is.*

But, of course, Atticus kept these thoughts to himself. "Please . . . sir." And lifting both hands now in worshipful gesture, Atticus took a deep breath and shouted at the utmost register of his vocal range: "*Apluga T'baccy. Wannachaw!*"

"—" the driver muttered when the last of the echoes died and the "Brides-to-Be" gasped at the strength of Atticus's devotion. Even the team of six were agi-

tated and one, the pie-bald bay, undoubtedly wishing to add its own devotionals to the moment, passed and extraordinary intense amount of intestinal effluvium.

"Oh sir, please," one of the "Ladies" pleaded, "give him achaw."

Caught in the paralyzing mist, Atticus could only feebly repeat: "*Apluga T'baccy. Wannachaw*" as the man looked down at the portion of deity he still held in a vise-like grip.

"Wall, which is it? Apluga or achaw?"

"*Apluga?*" Atticus was confused by the question. "*T'baccy, Wannachaw?*"

The *Staged coach* tilted noticeable toward the depot as the entire compliment of "Brides-to-Order" filled the windows to bestow piteous glances upon him.

"Gawd a'mighty!" the driver bellowed.

"Pray, sir," one of the crinoline-stiff ladies beseeched, "have you no mercy? Novice though he may be, cannot you see how he suffers for want? I plead his case onto you, sir — give him a chaw."

And Atticus, now the full mobility had been returned to him, fell to his knees and lifted his voice once more. "*Apluga T'baccy. Wannachaw!*"

The pie-bald horse glanced back in its traces, flicking its still-smoldering tail, as the Brides spewed forth earnest entreaties on his behalf. *Long may the Old Ones . . . and Apluga T'baccy approve of them.*

"Sir!"

"Please!"

"Do you not see his suffering?"

"G'awn'n give dah nipper achaw."

To which the driver only muttered incoherently, until —

"Fine," a feminine voice said, "he can have mine!"

"And mine."

"Yeh . . . ya tight-fist'd—!"

Atticus could not conceive — naturally, being male — but such was the magnanimous proposal of the stiff-bonneted and similarly-featured Brides, that he immediately felt a genuine stirring within his breast.

"*Wannachaw,*" he said with all humility.

And thus began the storm of benediction as piece after piece — no less than a half-dozen — of *Apluga T'baccy* rained down upon him and the platform on which he knelt.

Still in the guise of supplication, Atticus pulled a handkerchief from his coat pocket and, careful not to hold any too long, placed each twirled, gnarled and frequently gnawed-looking fragment upon his silk-draped palm.

"*Wannachaw,*" he said when the last of the fragments had been gathered and all tied into a bundle. "*Wannachaw, Apluga T'baccy.*"

"Yes, dear," one of the women said. "We know."

"*Wannachaw,*" he added once more and waved the ladies out of sight as the driver hollered to the horses and the *Staged coach* lumbered away into what now appeared to be nightfall.

He still had a great deal to learn about *The West,* Atticus thought as he set his posterior down upon his talus — the proximal row of bones of the tarsus, and breathed a sigh of resplendent relief.

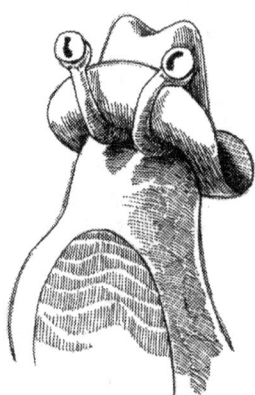

PLECOSTOMUS

"YOU think YOU are all powerful here, don't YOU?" he asked the silk-wrapped god-fragments in his hand. "YOU think YOU are all powerful here, don't YOU? Granted I have seen YOUR power over . . . the unsuspecting, but YOUR strength is nothing . . . it is as fragmented as your immortal shell . . . it is *nothing* compared to the might and majesty of the OLD ONES *I* serve.

"YOUR sovereignty will soon be over *Apluga T'baccy*! Soon — once I establish a foothold for the OLD ONES, YOU will see how ineffective YOU are.

"YOU will soon learn, O Fragmented-One, that reverse consumption is exactly contradictory to the *true* nature of supreme beings!"

(But he did mentally add: *Wannachaw!* just in case.)

"Oh, do give it a rest, Atticus."

Standing, Atticus glowered toward his brother at the same moment a slat-side cur, hereto unnoticed, realized that something, which had up until that moment been silent and anonymous, resided within the confines of the large wooden shipping crate that had been removed from the *Staged coach* along with the rest of Atticus's luggage. Narrow sides trembling with foreboding, the mongrel tucked its whip-like tail firmly between its hind legs and was gathering itself in for immediate flight . . . when Plecostomus reached through one of the crudely cut air-holes in the side of the crate and latched onto the animal. The feeding tentacle immediately refined its shape to accommodate the dog's overall proportions to a more easily digestible size.

So quick had his brother's actions been, that the dog hadn't had time to yelp one syllable before being consumed as a pre-dinner appetizer. Its brown eyes, still filled with bewilderment, continued to stare up at Atticus from where they sat in the dust of the platform.

"You always were a messy eater, Plecostomus," Atticus scolded.

Thus chided, his brother's tentacle swiped the eyes into the gathering dusk as if they were marbles.

"And *you,* my dear younger brother, could, I think, give oratory lessons to Mr. Phineas Taylor Barnum."

Snickering at his own wit, Plecostomus reached through another air-hole to release the carefully concealed latch atop the crate near the **THIS ELEVATION VERTICAL** stamp.

A moment later the great shimmering pustule-sack that was his elder brother, Plecostomus Uilleam Plughe, vomited forth from the crate's down-cushioned and satin-lined interior.

He, at least, had traveled in style and comfort; but by his first comment, one would have thought he'd suffered the same jarring indignities as Atticus.

"Dreadfully good to be out of there," Plecostomus chortled, elongating both his primary and secondary tentacle rings into an exaggerated yawn before extending a smile to his younger brother. Plecostomus took after their mother in looks, especially around the mouth.

"Goodness," he exclaimed, stretching his eye-stalk to its limit and turning, first right, then left, then behind to take in their surroundings. "Rather dismal place, isn't it? And this is what you dragged us from the comfort of our home? For *this*, Atticus . . . this *wasteland*?

"I must say, *little* brother, that I suspect Father will be anything but pleased when I wire him of it."

Atticus could feel the first faint fissures begin to form in his fraternal devotion. Long suffering beneath the yoke of his brother's senior standing in the family hierarchy, Atticus tightened his grip on the *Apluga T'baccy* (*Wannachaw*) and for the first time in his life, challenged the time-honored tradition. This was, after all, *The West*, where the standards and principles of the cultured East were discarded for the sake of Rugged Individualism.

In *The West* — or so he'd overheard the Brides say to one another while he was still in the Fragmented One's hallucinogenic grip — *'the men were men, and sheep were frightened.'*

Therefore, he could either be as an *Eastern* sheep or become a *Western* man!

Atticus chose the latter.

"When you do wire father, Plecostomus," Atticus said as he lifted the silken bundle toward his brother's face, "be sure to mention that *I* alone have secured the great Eldritch expansion westward, by single-handedly ensnaring and maintaining what may well be the only fragments left of *The West's* singular deity, *Apluga T'baccy*.

"*Wannachaw!*"

Panting with barely-contained zeal, Atticus watched his brother's eye-stalk lengthen until it was a mere inch from the silken bundle. The bulbous, gelatinous eye — the color of a bright summer's sky — narrowed.

"Are you sure?" Plecostomus asked.

"Sure? Of what?" Atticus doubly asked as he stepped back from his brother's all too probing eye and impertinent question.

"That what you hold in your hand is, in fact, all that remains of this western . . . god?"

Atticus's lips formed themselves into a tight, and what he hoped, bloodless line. "Of course, I am. Why would you even inquire?"

Without verbal answer, Plecostomus swung his eye-stalk toward the *Stagedcoach* Depot and gently tapped an advertisement that had been pasted to the front of the building just to the right of the chalkboard schedule.

So gentle was his brother's touch that barely a half-dozen shingles fell from the depot's roof. But Atticus barely noticed as he took a step closer to the sign and felt his liver go cold — which was an anatomic reaction he had never experienced until that moment.

OL' DOMINION T'BACCY

The first line read.

Prime Virginia cut — smoke cured and aged to perfection
5-cents loose
3-cents a plug
ASK FOR OL' DOMINION AT YOUR LOCAL TOBACCO ESTABLISHMENT

Directly beneath was another, smaller sign — pasted diagonally across the bottom of the first and done in bold, block letters, obviously hand-drawn:

Ol' Dominion for sale at C.D. Ward's Tobaccotarium and Hard-wear Emporium #6 Main Street, Upstairs.

"It would appear, *little* brother," Plecostomus chortled gibberishly and with such unrestrained glee that another dozen shingles left their place on the roof, "that you most certainly do *not* have all the fragments of this most segmented deity. *CHORTLE! CHORTLE!*"

Atticus's fingers tightened on the silk as he raised it to his lips.

"Why didn't you *say* something?" He hissed to the bundled god.

"Perhaps it's smarter than you gave it credit," Plecostomus, always *helpful* suggested as he shambled forward. "Even if it is only a *western* god living among uneducated savages and in an environment that seems more well suited to the inhabitants of solitary church yards instead of those who still practice inhalation at regular intervals . . . it is, supposedly, an ancient creature which has — unlike our own venerated MASTERS who prefer the anonymity of fog-shrouded coastlines and ill-conceived dwellings of dark wood and altered angles — deemed it necessary for its survival to co-exist with those it means to subjugate.

"Either that," Plecostomus added, "or it's a very clumsy deity and slipped somewhere in one of the other dimensions which caused it to fall into ours whereupon it shattered into, oh, shall we be conservative and say a few million pieces?"

"A few *million*?" Atticus now felt the chill which had invaded his liver consume the whole of his lower digestive tract.

"Which means, dearest brother," Plecostomus continued as he tapped one tentacle against Atticus's chest, "you have a bit more hunting and gathering to do before this . . ." His eye-stalk glanced over Atticus's shoulder. ". . . *land* is suitable for colonization.

"Don't you think?"

Atticus expletived most vehemently and would have hurled the silk-bundled deity into the pitch black *western* night (which was much darker than any night he'd seen in the East) . . . had that not meant he'd then be forced to walk out into that same inky blackness to fetch it back.

Any god — or piece thereof — was, in fact, better in the hand, then the brush.

Especially considering how many pieces of *Apluga T'baccy* there were left to find.

"*Wannachaw,*" he added miserably.

"Whatever," Plecostomus said, turning his attentions toward the town — if the double line of slap-sided wooden buildings huddled together like frightened children a scant hundred yards further down the rutted dirt road could candidly be called a *town*. There was evidence of life, however in the sounds of tinkering music accompanied by frequent masculine shouts and/or feminine squeals. Atticus could not tell if the shouts and squeals were from pain or pleasure . . . but they, as nothing else before, were reminiscent of home.

And the torments inflicted by the OLD ONES upon their servants.

It was such a strong memory that a duet of brotherly sighs drifted through the darkness — "Ah."

"Well, much as I hate to offer you anything in the way of tribute, little brother," Plecostomus said, "it does appear that you may have found perhaps the single western settlement where this *Apluka Tobaccus—*"

"*Apluga T'baccy,*" Atticus corrected. "*Wannachaw.*"

Plecostomus *gallumped* deep in his throat, as he always did when he thought he was being mocked or made light of.

"As – I – Was – Saying." His brother lowered his eye-stalk directly into Atticus's face. "*Gallump.* You may have indeed found the one settlement where this god feels the most secure . . . for why else would there be a public proclamation proclaiming its whereabouts?"

As was their custom throughout childhood, Atticus's first inclination was to disagree with Plecostomus's assumption . . . until he realized his brother had actually paid him a rare compliment, and thus had no choice but to agree.

With very little effort, Atticus felt his chest again swell with pride.

"I concur most readily, dear brother."

But as the words left Atticus's lips, a wicked grin appeared on Plecostomus's. "Then I assume you know exactly what needs to be done now?"

Atticus felt his chest deflate. "Uh. We telegraph Mother to tell her we've arrived safely?"

The grin on his brother's lips lengthened into a smirk. "This is why, sweet child, that I was sent along with you. *First*, Atticus, we must find this C. D. Ward and obtain *all* the pieces of this *Alpaca-Tabba* . . . and do not attempt to correct me again, little brother . . . that he has; *Second* we proceed to beat this fragmented deity's petitioner severely about the head and shoulders until he either convinces us that we have, in fact, *all* the segments or he gives us the location, or locations, where the rest may be found.

"*Third* I dispose of the Mr. Wards remains." Plecostomus belched up a wad of gray-brown fur. "Pardon. Dog never did agree with me. Now let me see, where was I?"

"*Fourth*," Atticus said helpfully.

"Ah, yes . . . *Fourth*, we telegraph Mother and tell her we've arrived safely. Do you agree?"

Atticus nodded, miserable as he felt the reins of power being pulled from his grasp. The reins possibly — and he

tightened his grip on the silken bundle — but *not* what he held in his hand. Not now . . . not ever.

"And finally," Plecostomus said, reveling in his triumph, "I think a full hot meal, or several, and then you'll need to find suitable lodgings for our stay. Do you think this settlement might have a cistern or something similar? I'm fairly parched from all this heat."

"It's not the heat," Atticus answered humbly as they began to walk — and shamble, respectively — toward #6 Main Street. Upstairs. "It's the lack of humidity."

Plecostomus *gallumped* for the third time that night and nudged Attics brusquely. "Parasite," he growled, gurgling with fraternal delight.

"Chrysalis," Atticus chimed back, indebted that their Mother had made word games a mandatory pastime when they were growing up.

"Curculio," Plecostomus fired back.

"Emmet."

"Pismire."

"Leveret."

"Cicala."

"Slug!"

While his brother thought of a suitable riposte, Atticus held aloft the silk-wrapped bundle into the dark night. There was no need, he realized, not to give deference to the NEW GOD even as he and his brother went forth to pave the way for the OLD.

The West did appear large enough to accommodate all.

And if it wasn't and a glorious other-dimensional war was to ensue, there was no reason to make irreparable injuries to what might very well be the victor. It was, after all, a land of limitless possibilities.

Wannachaw!

The End of PART I.

PART II: Water Rites . . . coming soon

THE COW-MEN OF COBURN

by Will Murray

illustrated by P.D. Weincek

After six miles of tracking, they found the stray standing off the trail, howling at the full moon like it was half wolf.

"There she be," said Clay Allison.

"Yup," rejoined Walter Wayne of the Cattleman's Association. "There she be."

"Her brand should tell the tale, if there is any tale in need of tellin'."

"Reckon so," said Walt.

They approached the cow casually. There was no hurry. They had come a long ways over northern Arizona day and night for two weeks now. An Arizona Ranger and an agent of the Cattlemen's Protective Association, searching for a herd of beef that had set out from the Triangle **C** ranch and simply got swallowed up in the vastness of the Overholser Trail. Three hundred head of cattle and twenty-two men that should have made Abeline the month before.

Yet not a word or an outrider. No trace of man nor beast.

Until they came upon the tracks of a stray. . . .

Dismounting, the pair approached the lone cow from behind. It had fallen silent. At the sound of their boots, its tail flicked once. It did not turn its head to look at them.

They started at the hind end, patting its bony flanks and looking for the telltale brand.

"Here," whispered Clay. Walt joined him.

"Looks like a **C** in a triangle," he muttered, squinting through the moonlight at the burned-in brand.

"Look again."

"That's sure a **C**. But it's more'n a star than a triangle . . ."

"Never heard of any **C**-in-a-star brand," Clay said flintily. "Wouldn't take much to obliterate a triangle by burnin' a star over it."

"Damn. Rustled."

Clay looked over the shoulders on his way to the head. "Not yet skin and bones, but she's gettin' there . . ."

"He. It's a steer."

"Pardon me for not lookin'." Clay's voice trailed off. He was quiet a full minute. The steer gave voice to a pitiful burble of a sound.

When the Ranger spoke again, his voice was thin as a moonbeam. "Walt. Step up this way a minute . . ."

Walt joined him. He looked into the steer's low-hanging face, and swallowed several times before he got out a croak that might have been an oath, or no actual word at all.

"Look familiar?" Clay asked.

"Yeah," Walt muttered. He looked into the steer's sad green eyes and they stared back at him for the longest space of time.

"Do you want to do the duty, or must I?" Clay asked at last.

Thick of voice, Walt said, "It's my responsibility. I'll do it."

Walter Wayne stalked back to his mount, and unshipped a shotgun from its saddle sleeve. He broke it, ascertained two shells were in place and snapped the weapon back together.

His face was fixed as he walked up to the now-quiet steer. He didn't hesitate. He stuck the double barrel behind the bovine skull and, without preamble or sentiment, let loose with both thundering barrels. Matter splattered.

The steer wobbled on suddenly-quivering legs. Its back legs began to cave, but the forelegs collapsed before them.

The steer fell smack onto its face.

"We should bury it," Clay stated.

"We should. But we won't." Reloading his shotgun, Walt Wayne methodically blew the steer's face off.

"Now it's settled all decent-like," he said.

Without a word, they remounted and started north. The man with the star rode a Steeldust stallion. His sidekick forked a strawberry Roan. Twenty years spanned the difference between their ages, but sun and wind and windblown sand had weathered their seamed faces until they had taken on the look of brothers, although they were not even kin.

It was a long time before either spoke. More than a hour by moon reckoning, and over a mile.

"You work with cows all your damn life." Walt muttered. "You rope 'em, brand 'em, feed 'em, and you think you know the critters. And then this . . ."

The older Ranger nodded sagely. "My granddaddy used to have a sayin'. 'Cows is cows.' "

Walt grunted. "Can't say that no more . . ."

"No, I can't. And Granddaddy's long gone. Good thing he didn't live to see this. It would have upset him something powerful."

"Ain't doin' my disposition no damn good, neither. Not to mention my stomach."

"What was it like? Shootin' the poor beast like that."

"What do you think?" Walt said sav-

agely. "Like murderin' your own damn flesh and blood. Ain't no damn difference."

They fell silent again.

A quarter mile further along, Walt spoke again. "What torments me most was the last time I laid eyes on him, he weren't no steer. He had all his natural equipment."

Clay Allison shuddered. They rode onward.

Dawn came. They had no thought of sleep, or bedding down. The Superstition Mountains were far behind them when they came upon the rider and his horse, flat to the ground, their bones picked clean by carrion vultures. One still lingered.

Clay raised his Colt Peacemaker to the burning sky and let off a shot.

The vulture spread black wings as if in no hurry and stubbornly refused to desert his post until they were practically on top of the mound of bones and leather and flannel that had once been a man and his mount. It winged off on lazy pinions.

Dismounting, they inspected the remains.

"Appears to have been dead a week or more. . . ." Clay pronounced.

"Maybe so."

There was no recognizing the rider. His face was a shield of yellowing bone, his Mexican sombrero tipped forward over his face. A pair of smoked glasses lay beside him.

"Looks like the birds left him some hair," said Clay, plucking off the hat.

The hair was like straw, dirty and windstirred. A whipscorpion scuttled from sight. But that wasn't what froze the two men in their boots.

Sticking out from the bony forehead were a pair of short thick horns.

"The Devil hisself!" Walt exploded.

"Nope, it's some trick of a joke," snorted Clay. Unclasping his knife, he dug at the horns. The macabre scraping of steel on bone came back like a warning growl.

"Embedded good," he grunted.

"Looks like you miscalculated somewhat," Walt muttered.

"Looks like," Clay agreed.

"What would the Devil be doin' out here?"

"Good place for him, considering it's hotter'n the hinges of Hell. But that ain't the Devil. The Devil can't die. And this poor soul is plain defunct."

"What is it, then?"

"Search me. Mystery of the desert. Not our concern."

"You don't suppose he — it's — tied up with that missin' herd?"

Clay remounted, saying, "If it is, I want no part of it."

Walt joined him. "It's still our jobs."

"And we'll do 'em. But between you and me, I'm losing all appetite for this whole deal . . ."

They rode on.

"I've worked in double-rigged country and in center-fire country," Walt Wayne muttered darkly. "Never happened upon sights such as I have seen on this day. Cows with uncow faces. Dead men with Lucifer horns. What deviltry will ride up next?"

"That's what worries me, too," the Arizona Ranger said flatly.

For the remainder of the day neither man spoke. It was as if all the words had been sucked out of them by the dry heat.

Hours passed in which only the creaking of saddle leather and the monotonous crunch and clink of shod hooves on sand and stone broke the silence.

They were passing out of the low desert with its manlike Saguaro cactus and scattered scrub into a rugged zone where painted cliffs and tabletop mesas twisted the arid landscape into something even more forbidding. Petrified trees lay scattered about as if blasted by primeval lightning. Jumping cactus predominated.

Farther along, a lone rider presented himself at the top of a painted promontory less than a quarter-mile distant. He perched bareback on an Appaloosa pony.

"Looks like a Hopi," Walt remarked, eyeing his dramatic outline.

"Look again. He's wearing a serape."

"So he is. But that's gotta be a Hopi, or maybe an Apache medicine man. Look at that high-falutin' Injun headdress he's got on."

The Indian gestured broadly with one arm. He pointed north. Then with a majestic sweep of one blanketed arm, pointed back they way they had come. He stabbed three times with a medicine stick decorated with feathers and topped by a human skull.

Clay said, "He's makin' sign. Can't you read it?"

"Looks like he's urgin' us to go back."

"No reservation up ahead that I know of . . ." Clay mused. "Just badlands hills."

"Then he's got no right stickin' his horns into our affairs."

They continued on. After a while, the Indian disappeared from sight.

"How do you think he keeps them things balanced on his head?" Clay wondered.

"Got me. In my travels, I've come across Injuns wearing cow horns and buffalo horns. Never did see one sportin' Texas longhorns like that."

Clay chuckled dryly. "Well, Walt, now you can say you've seen just about everything!"

"Somethin' right unnatural about a human head carrying that much weight like that . . ." Walt opined darkly.

"What's your point?"

"That buzzard-picked rider back a ways . . ."

"What about him?"

Walt swallowed, then forced the words out. "Well, if I come out and just say it, you're gonna call me a damn' fool," he said hotly.

"Come out and say it anyways," Clay invited.

"Them devil horns of his. They looked more like the equipment you normally see on a Holstein."

Clay Allison said nothing. The comparison obviously troubled his thinking.

Dusk brought them to the outskirts of a town. It loomed up ahead, a cluster of closely-packed wood-frame buildings dominated by none.

A crude sign by the side of the sand-spit road read: COBURN. NO LAW, NO CHINAMEN, NO INJUNS, NO PREACHERS, NO WOMEN, NO COWBOYS ALLOWED. TURN BACK NOW.

"What's left?" Walt wondered.

Tucking his star into a vest pocket, Clay Allison said, "Us."

"You do all the talkin' then."

"I aim to."

They rode in, their shooting irons hanging cool and convenient at their sides.

Walt crinkled up his nose. "Sure got that cow-town air," he ventured.

"Yup."

Except for a Palomino tied up at a watering trough, the boardwalk was deserted.

As they rode past it, a deep voice was heard to say, "Turn back."

"Who said that?" Walt hissed.

"Vamoose," the deep voice repeated.

They looked around. The only pair of eyes that met theirs were the sad dark ones of the tied Palomino. It turned away. The same deep voice said, "You were warned."

Somewhere a cowbell began ringing violently. It sounded like an alarm.

Out of a doorway stepped a man. He strode down off the boardwalk on booted feet that seemed strangely narrow. His heels rang like hoof-beats. In the gathering dusk, they could spy a wide face decorated by broad distended nostrils under a ten gallon hat. His eyes were masked by a pair of smoked glasses.

"Clay, you notice what I'm noticin'?"

"Yup."

The man took up a position on the

street before them. He put hands on hips. Something gleamed on his chest in the dying red sunlight.

"You the law in Coburn?" Clay Allison demanded.

"There is no law in Coburn," the man returned. "Who be you?"

They rode right up to him until they could get a good look at his face. He was a substantial individual, his broad shoulders like two-by-fours. But it was the star pinned to his flannel chest that drew their gaze.

"Thought you said there was no law in Coburn," ventured Cliff.

"There ain't."

"Then what's that brass star on your chest?"

"Ain't no star. This be a pentacle."

"A which?" Walt sputtered.

"I am the Warder of Coburn. What be your business?"

Clay offered. "None, Warder. We're just riding through on our way north. Gonna join the Army and fight Apaches."

"You men look like cowboys. . . ."

"Not us," returned Clay promptly.

"Yeah," added Walt. "Lately, we're downright allergic to cows."

Behind his dark glasses the Warder of Coburn seemed to crinkle up his thick features in a frown.

"Mind your tongue," spat the Warder. "This be a cow-town."

"I can smell that," sniffed Walt. "Funny thing, though. You not toleratin' cowboys in a cow-town."

"No cowboys in Coburn. Only cowmen allowed."

"Well, we're neither species," Clay Allison returned evenly.

"Best you ride straight through and keep on going," the Warder snorted.

Walt asked, "We're thirsty. Is there a saloon?"

"We don't serve liquor in Coburn."

Clay forced a toothy smile. "Sasparilla then?"

"No sasparilla. Only milk. Fill your canteens from the trough and ride on."

"If'n you say so," Clay returned cheerfully.

He did the filling, pumping the well handle and passing the canteens to his saddle partner. Remounting, they continue on.

Eyes semed to be looking down at them from both sides of the street. Once, they caught sight of a woman's face. Smoky glasses obscured her eyes, too. As she hurried back indoors, they noticed that her bustle was strangely active.

Her dress kept jumping and twitching as if there was something under it trying to get out.

"Damn passin' strange," muttered Clay Allison.

Clearing the sunrise side of town, they cantered on. After casting careful glances behind them, they soon became convinced they were not being trailed.

Walt spat suddenly. "What in hell's a Warder if not the law?"

"Damned if I know."

"And who sports smoked glasses after sunset?"

"Damned if I know," Clay repeated.

"And what in blue tarnation is a pentacle?"

"The brand of Satan, if you ask me."

"Or a rustler's brand. Whole damn town smelled of cows. And whoever heard of a cow-town full of cowmen, but no cowboys allowed. Do the Apaches raise all chiefs and no bucks? It ain't natural."

"Yeah. Likely there's a herd somewhere's about."

"If so, we'll sniff it out."

The desert was far behind them now. This was badlands country. Upflung buttes overlooked deep ravines and arroyos. Box canyons large enough to swallow whole lakes became visible on the rising trail. There were thousand places to hide beef on the hoof, but no logical place to start searching.

They bedded down for the night. The moon rose like a lantern climbing a ladder.

Long about midnight, refreshed, Clay Allison shook his partner awake.

"Town should be asleep by now. Let's get to creepin' around."

They left their horses tethered to a petrified tree-trunk.

A midnight wind seemed to be carrying the earthy tang of cattle from the west. They picked their way in that direction.

"This is the most Godforsaken part of Arizony," Walt Wayne was muttering. "Nothin' but rimrock and declivities and all manner of misplaced stone. You need grass to bed down a herd."

"I smell cow."

"I smell cow too. But where are they?"

They followed the odor of cattle until it grew so distinct they were obliged to turn their sweaty neckerchiefs into face masks to help keep it out of their clogging nostrils.

It was the biggest barn either of them had ever seen. Possibly a dozen hay barns could have been encompassed within its long red confines.

They came up on the lee side of it. The big red barn stood in a flat canyon floor. At one end, above a double door large enough to admit ten buckboards rolling abreast of one another, someone had daubed a pentacle in white. Within it, a chalky letter **C**.

"Looks like we may have hit paydirt at last," Clay said tightly.

"Back East, I hear tell farmers paint what they call a Hex sign over their barns to ward off trouble."

The Ranger frowned. "What sort of trouble?"

"Everythin' from consumption to scalp-seekin' braves."

"Well, I smell cows but I don't see any. No honest cattleman stores his steers inside of a barn. Simple subtraction tells me we have found the lost Triangle **C** herd."

Walt surveyed his surroundings. "Not a lick of grass, neither," he muttered. "Ain't natural."

"Will you stop sayin' that? Match you for who takes a look-see."

Walt won the coin toss. He hitched his gunbelt tighter and clambered down toward the barn.

His Colt drawn and cocked, Clay followed his clumsy progress with sun-squint eyes.

Walt came back not ten minutes later, several shades paler, both eyes round as the lunar orb above.

"Well?" wondered Clay.

"There's a cow in there, all right."

"Only one?"

"Don't talk so disappointed like. It was the biggest, damnedest cow you ever did see."

"Talk sense."

"It was just a'sittin' there, eyes shut, asleep to the world, forelegs folded in its lap, tail curled around it like no cow I ever beheld."

"What brand?"

Walt seemed not to hear. He kept talking. "I've seen ring-tailed raccoons, heard tall tales of ring-tailed wampus cats, and I've even been told that there's a ring-tailed monkey out there in the bigger world. But I ain't never before encountered a ring-tailed cow."

"What brand?" the Ranger repeated.

Walt starred off into space. He licked dry lips. "Clay, I gotta tell you one thing. My whole entire world's been turned upside down. Cows ain't cows. Leastways, not no more."

"If I didn't know better, I'd gunslap you for a common drunk," Clay Allison spat back. "What's eatin' you?"

"Truthfully, I ain't been the same since that pile-up I had with a loco steer and a Joshua tree which busted up my kneecap near to five years ago. Couldn't make a hand no more on the range, so I settled for becomin' a cattleman's agent. Let me tell you, life was sure simpler when all a man had to worry about was a calf gettin' caught up in devil-wire and rememberin' where you left your poncho when it commenced a'thunderin'."

"I didn't ask you for your biography. All I want to know —"

"I ain't got the words, Clay. You'd better go see for yourself. My sense of reality has been plumb insulted."

"All right, I will. You guard my back."

Clay started down toward the barn, .44-.40 Colt handy in his fist.

"Don't wake it, whatever you do," Walt hissed after him. "No tellin' what it'll do to yuh."

Walt Wayne methodically whetted his knife on the hard heel of his boot as he waited. The moon stayed out, full and round as a silver dollar. Not a scrap of cloud troubled the night sky.

" 'Cows is cows,' so the sayin' goes," he told himself. "Well, that particular nostrum ain't worth a plugged nickel now. . . ."

He watched his partner creep down toward big barn doors, slip within, and grimly returned to his knife sharpening.

Arizona Ranger Clay Allison returned shortly with his face as stiff as a scarecrow's after a hard rain. His eyes were like gopher holes — dead hollows in his skull.

"We'll need a shotgun," he said thickly. "Probably both of 'em."

"For what?"

"To kill it."

Walt Wayne was silent a long moment. "I was kinda hopin' you'd come back to say it weren't really real. A statue like the golden calf that Moses threw down, or an old Aztec idol, or something that made a little bit of sense."

The Arizona Ranger shook his head. "It's real. I smelt it. I watched its ribs work like a bellows. It was breathin' all right. It's got no right sitting there like a man but looking like a cow. No justification on God's great green footstool. But I saw it and you saw it and now we got to kill it."

They trudged back to their horses. The surrounding blue and gray and lavender cliff striations had merged into a single leaden hue. Petrified trees cast stark shadows.

"What do you reckon it's worth?" Clay asked the cattlemen's agent at length.

"Our lives if it wakes up on us."

"No. I mean at a beef gather."

"Gotta weigh upwards of 20,000 pounds. That's a powerful pile of beefsteaks. Worth as much as a small silver mine maybe. Not to mention all that fresh milk. Udders looked full to burstin'."

Clay nodded. "I think it's getting ready to calve."

"Can't have that. It would upset the balance of nature."

"That's why we gotta do what we gotta damn well do. And we gotta do it tonight."

"Amen — not that I'm a prayin' sort of cuss."

"I take your meaning."

The horses were nervous when they reached them. Even here, the reek of cow was overpowering.

Clay Allison gentled his Steeldust as he unshipped his shotgun. Wayne did the same. They began checking their weapons and stuffing their pockets with extra Double-O shells.

"What if this don't do the job?" Walt wondered.

"Don't think that way. The Almighty Himself may be counting on us."

"He sure picked a novel way to test a couple of former cowhands."

They started back.

Walt muttered, "I sure hope this ain't it."

"Ain't what?" Clay asked.

"Them Latter Days they talk about it in the Good Book."

"I don't recall any mention of prodigious cows in the Bible."

"Well, there was somethin' cowlike and ungodly supposed to emerge from the sea in the Latter Days. . . ."

"You're thinking of Leviathan, Walt. Or maybe Rahab."

"Weren't Rahab nothin' but a no-account whore?"

"That's a different Rahab altogether."

"Naw, I'm recollectin' somethin' else entirely. Somethin' horned and fearsome, just like that thing heathen in the barn."

"There were said to be giants in the old days," Clay allowed. "'Course, this is now."

Walter Wayne erupted like a geyser. "Behemoth! That's it. That thing's just gotta be the Behemoth ol' Job wrote about. I can practically recite him from memory." His voice grew portentous:

"See, besides you I made Behemoth,
that feeds on grass like an ox.
He carries his tail like a cedar;
the sinews of his thighs are like cables.
His bones are like tubes of bronze;
his frame is like iron rods."

Clay frowned darkly. "Behemoth wasn't supposed to rise up in the Latter Days. It was something else. A dragon, I think. Or some such monster of old."

"That's good then," Walt said, relieved. "For if that barn Behemoth ain't a sign of the Latter Days, we got us half a chance."

They picked their way among rocks and ossified branches, making almost no sound. If it weren't for the moonlight, they would not have spied the tracks. Hoofprints. Several pair.

"Looks like five, maybe six cows," Walt muttered, bending down to read their pattern. "Funny . . ."

"What?"

"They ain't quite matched up right."

"What do you mean, Walt?"

"Well, look, if this here's the front hooves, where's the hindquarters set? And why are they walkin' every which way like that?"

"What are you saying?"

"Nothin'. But I ain't never heard tell of no two-legged cattle."

Clay snorted derisively. "No such animals."

"Pray you're right," Walt muttered, unconvinced.

A quarter mile along, they came within spitting distance of the big red barn. Rocks and escarpments lay all around them, gray and spectral in the moonlight.

"Know any good prayers?" Clay asked Walt.

Walt rubbed his chin thoughtfully. "Maybe I can summon up what else the Book of Job said of great Behemoth." He closed his eyes and began a lofty recitation:

"Who can capture him by his eyes,
or piece his nose with a trap?
Can you put a rope into his nose,
or pierce through his cheek with a gaff?
Will the traders bargain for him?
Will the merchants divide him up?
Once you but lay a hand upon him,
no need to recall any other conflict!"

Clay ruminated a moment, then said, "Not exactly comforting, is he?"

"Maybe it's just one of them Biblical admonitions . . ." Walt said slowly. "Like the parable of the Trojan —"

Abruptly, several behatted heads reared up before them. A hard knot of men formed, blocking their path.

"Cowboys," Clay hissed.

"Naw, rustlers. Look at the size of them hats. Made for makin' shade on their dishonest faces."

They wore hats of ridiculous proportions. Ten gallon hats. Mexican Sombreros. Beneath the wide brims of their outlandish headgear, every pair of eyes was masked by smoked glasses.

And in their midst glinted a strange star.

"It's that Warder feller," Walt muttered.

"Halt," the familar deep voice of the Warder of Coburn announced.

They complied, their shotguns held only slightly downward, ready for instant elevation and subsequent action.

Clay asked, "That you, Warder?"

Came a bestial growl: "Drop your weapons to the ground."

"Claw sky your own damned selves!" Walt snapped back. "We ain't in your milk-liver cow-town no more!"

That was all it took. Orange flame speared the night.

Shotgun blasts roared in response. Hot lead spanged and careened off rock. Men scattered, breaking in all directions.

It was all over in a quarter minute.

From behind a rock, Walt Wayne hissed, "Clay? You still breathin'?"

"Breathing, but bleeding."

"Damn. How bad?"

"Slug perforated my Stetson. Creased my scalp some."

"I think they high-tailed it."

"The live ones, at any rate."

Emerging from shelter, they reconnoitered. Acrid powder haze obscured everything in sight. They fanned it away with their hats.

Three cow-men of Coburn lay sprawled in the trail. Blood spattered everything for yards around. One gave a strange lowering groan before the death rattle in his throat foretold his mortal expiration.

Under the moonlight, his eyes, shorn of smoked glasses, gleamed wetly.

"Damanation!" The profanity was torn from Walter Wayne's lips.

The eyes were dark and sad and familar to both men. They lacked proper whites, but they were otherwise unmistakable.

Walt nudged the corpse with the toe of his boot. "This one's got cow sorta eyes . . ."

Clay called back. "This one, too. They all do. And these hats were built for concealing horns. They got them too."

"That ain't the least of it. Check out their feet. They ain't got any."

The gunmen weren't wearing boots. Regulation boots would have rejected them. For instead of normal feet, they were hooved.

"I read that Satan comes outfitted with cloven feet," Clay Allison said slowly.

"The Devil ain't no heifer. These here are cattle feet. That's why them tracks back yonder went everywhich a way. Weren't no cattle. They were . . ." He scratched his cheek thoughtfully. "What the hell are these conglomerate brutes?"

"They're exactly what they called themselves," the Ranger pronounced grimly. "Cow-men."

"Cow-men," Walt grunted. "Sons of steers and born of no woman. Small wonder they had a mean-on against cowboys. But where could they have come from?"

"Don't know. But if I were to guess, I'd guess that cow-bomination in the barn fixin' to calve might be our answer."

"All the more reason to be done with it."

They moved on, more wary now.

"If anything pops up, don't ask fool questions. Just shoot it dead," Clay warned.

"You don't need to tell an old cow-hand twice . . ."

Climbing down a tumble of rocks, the two partners made their way to the flat space in which the red barn from Hell sat silent in the moonlight.

Clay took the lead. Walt Wayne followed at a respectful distance. No sense being bunched up should gunfire erupt from the surrounding rocks.

Adjusting their bandana handkerchiefs to protect mouth and nose, they advanced, throwing cautious glances to the high ground. A rifle whanged somewhere. The sound was repeated. Rock dust kicked up. But both men had thrown themselves flat at the sound.

They got up, conned their surroundings. Darkness defeated them.

Creeping forward, they fought against gagging at the stink of cow.

From behind the barn, a man stepped out. In the moonlight, his hat sat on his head like it was meant for a giant. Silver effulgence reflected off his smoked glasses. He lifted a flintlock rifle to his shoulder.

It blew fire and smoke in calamitous quantities. But otherwise had no noticeable effect.

Dropping his shotgun, Clay Allison pulled his Colt, cocked it and began flinging lead. His bullets flew true. The cow-man was knocked off his narrow hooves. There was a brief twitching of something thin and whiplike.

"Lord have mercy!" Walt exploded. "He's got a tail too!"

"Now you know why that Coburn woman's skirt was actin' up."

More gunfire erupted. All of it ineffectual.

"They gotta be the worst shots goin'!" Walt snorted.

"What would you expect? They're more cow than man."

"That's plumb debatable," Walt snapped.

They reached the barn. The double door was ajar, just as they had left it.

Walt suddenly grabbed Clay by the sleeve. "You don't suppose —"

"Suppose what?" Clay hissed back.

"All those admonitions ol' Job offered up about leavin' Behemoth well alone weren't some injunction against man worryin' beef?"

"Come again?"

"Don't it say somewheres in the Good Book that the meek will inherit the Earth?" Walt persisted. "What if they meant . . . cows?"

"You're loco!"

"What's meeker'n a cow, I ask? Answer me that!"

"I didn't take up wearing this star to surrender dominion over the Earth," Clay snapped. "We got a job to do, and we're doing it. Come on!"

Walt lifted troubled eyes to the starlit sky, and prayed, "Lord, I ask your sincere forgiveness if I'm going agin' the Great Plan . . ."

One at a time, they slipped in.

"Like Jonah goin' into the whale's gullet," Walt muttered.

"Count of three," Clay whispered. "One — Two — Three!"

Four blazing barrels emptied into the half gloom of the barn.

Walt unloosed five shots from his Colt while Clay hastily reloaded both shotguns. He never got a chance to finish the job.

Gunfire cracked among the rimrocks. But it was soon drowned out by a low sound, proceeding from within the cavernous barn. It began as a tentative moan, swelled into a earsplitting groan and soon rose into a bellow so prodigious that it rattled the plank sides of the barn like an earthquake.

"We dadgum woke her!" Walt shouted.

"We still gotta scrag that Trojan," Clay snapped. Tossing a shotgun, he said, "Here's yours."

The ungodly bellowing lifted and lifted into the sky. A great smashing cacophony as of a forest turning to kindling vied to outrival it. Splintered planks rattled down the sloping roof, raining down on them.

Ducking lumber, Walt shrilled, "She's bustin' loose! Flung her bossy head clear up through the roof! It's Job's judgment for sure!"

"Shoot! Shoot, consarn you!"

Eyes squeezed shut, Walt unloaded both barrels.

Splintered moonbeams outlined a heaving bellows of a piebald torso, the madly switching tail of many-colored rings, and the horrible stink of commingled blood and milk assaulted their senses.

From the rocks, lifting voices cried a single half-decipherable word. A blanketed figure stood strong against the night. On his head, a pair of outspread horns that would have done justice to a longhorn steer shook with rage.

"*C'WTHULHU, yah! C'WTHULHU, yah!*"

"What's he bellerin'?" Walt asked.

"Don't know. Don't care. Give me shootin' room!"

"Must be Apache," Walt muttered. "Sounds like their lingo."

The ground under their feet began to

vibrate. It gave up a sound. Or was it coming from the hills?

The earth trembled and shook. Soon the drumming racket resolved into a sound that all cowmen dreaded.

"Stampede!" Clay cried. "Get clear!"

They dispersed with alacrity, from the vicinity of the barn.

Walt made for the rocks. He reached them on boots that barely touched ground. He looked back, mouth hanging slack and surprised. He turned. He could spy his partner trying to climb the crumbling base of a sandstone cliff. Clay was like an ant attempting to scale loose mound of dirt. Despite valiant effort, he fell back again and again.

For a long moment, the tableau etched itself into Walter Wayne's brain.

There was the red barn. Its roof gambrel was stove open. From the shattered cavity, a great horned head, crazed of eye and bovine of countenance, threshed and bellowed, throwing off spittle.

But that wasn't the sight that froze Walt Wayne's immortal soul.

Down from the badlands hills came a thundering herd of steers, their remorseless hooves pounding out a path of destruction.

Like a many-horned wave, it washed toward the big red barn. Eyes red with the murder lust, nostrils distended wildly they charged. And neither man nor God could turn them from their goal. Implacable, unavoidable, they came on as a many-legged force of nature made one, rage-filled voices lifted to join the distress cry of their lowering overlord.

At the last, ultimate second, the herd broke, parting, making two streams. Hide and hair and hooves rattled by like a freight train from Perdition.

And caught up in that cascade of beef, transfixed yet squirming like a human sacrifice, Clay Allison was carried aloft on the prongs of the lead longhorn.

All while the moaning bellow of Great Mother C'wthulhu shook the silver moon in a shivering sky.

Yet that was not the toughest part. Walt Wayne had been men gored and trampled before. It was never any easier to behold. But this was different.

Racing by, the frightened faces of the mad steers burned into his awestruck brain. Men who know cattle learn to see them individually. Men who work cattle get to know their traits, their vagaries, their idle moods.

No two cows look alike. As fast as they drummed past, Walter Wayne could spot the unmistakable earmarks of personality in those red-eyed semi-bovine faces.

Faces he had known from his trail days. Faces that belonged to the lost cowboys of the Triangle **C**. Faces like the one he had blown off a stray steer to avoid offending the sight of God and man less than a day before. *Faces like the dour, elongated visage that had formerly belonged to his cousin Matt, one of the lost trail-hands of the Triangle C outfit . . .*

Somehow, he got away. By some miracle Walter Wayne threaded his way through unforgiving rock and horn-headed demi-men and circled back to his hobbled horse.

Wayne rode off as if the very Devil were in pursuit, waving a red-hot branding iron.

"Cows ain't cows no more," he sobbed. "And cowboys aren't what they used to be neither. I'm all done with cattle. Ol' Job had it right. The meek are right now inheritin' the Earth. Human-kind is plumb ruined!"

Around the Bend in the Trail . . .

Three blazing novelets of six-shootin' action in the next issue of *Weird Trails, the Magazine of Supernatural Cowboy Stories*:

A new Buck Eldritch adventure of ancient secrets
"RETURN TO FUGGOTH FLATS"
by M.M. MOAMRATH

They couldn't make out a word he said. That only made things worse.
Find out why in
"THE GIBBERING GALOOT"
by PETRONIUS PEMMICAN, Ph.D.

Completely rewritten from that pretentious version in *The Dial,*
here is the real story of
"THE WASTE LAND"
by TEX STRAIGHTSHOOTER ELIOT

Plus the exciting conclusion to "Trouble at Cthulhu Canyon" by Ron Goulart, a new "Riverrun Ranch" story by James Joyce, and more thrilling ghostly action by Lee "Tex" Weinstein, P.D. "Tex" Cacek, Col. George "Tex" Scithers, Howard Philips "Rhode Island" Lovecraft, Robert Leslie Bellem, Seabury Quinn, Bassett Morgan, E. Hoffmann Price, and J. Hieronymous Hackwort.

THE ONE THAT GOT AWAY

by Mike Resnick

When cowboys sit around the campfire and tell their mournful stories, they talk of Billy Nightfall, who was shot in the back by the woman he loved, and Texas Slade McBride, who worked for seven years breaking the meanest broncs anyone ever saw, and when he'd finally saved up enough money to send for the mail-order bride he'd lost his heart to, got rip-roaring drunk and blew everything he was going to spend on her in a crooked card game. They tell of Westerly Wilson, whose betrothed left him for a fast-talking snake-oil salesman and how his bitterness turned him to a life of crime as a Californy real estate broker.

But the saddest story of all is the story of Howlin' Jack Dawkins.

Nobody knew where he came from. Some say he'd worked alongside Hopalong Cassidy at the Bar-20, other say he'd spent time with Curly Bill Bannerman at the Lazy S. But his tragic tale really begins the day he hired on at the Bar Sinister.

Jack had a way with cattle and sheep. One look from him and they huddled together and did exactly as he wanted. No one could remember ever seeing him fire a shot or crack a whip; when Howlin' Jack glared at an animal, that was all the encouragement it needed.

He didn't have no use for the bunkhouse. Kept everything he owned in his saddle bags, and said he preferred sleeping out under the night sky to layin' in a bed listening to everyone snoring.Besides, he seemed to be one of them guys who didn't need much sleep, because every morning when the others would wake up, there he'd be, squatting by the fire, ready to pour coffee for anyone who came by.

Every now and then, long about midday, he'd fall asleep in his saddle as he was riding along, but everyone just figured he'd been working too hard, and no one mentioned it except to tease him in a good-natured way. They all liked him, and he got along just fine with them, but he couldn't help feeling that there was something lacking in his life, though he didn't know what it was — and then came the fateful day that he rode into town to pick up some supplies, and he saw the stagecoach from Wichita pulling in, and since he'd never seen anyone from a big sophisticated city before, he was kind of curious as to what they looked like and how they dressed, so he stuck around and watched them climb down out of the coach.

And that was when he first saw her. One look was all it took, and he'd lost his heart forever. Her name was Bunny Wigglesworth, and she had golden hair, and she'd been to some finishing school, whatever that is, back East, and she was on her way to Californy to visit an uncle or a cousin or some such who'd made his fortune out there.

Anyway, the second Jack saw her he felt like baying the moon, which wasn't the first time he'd ever had that urge, but it was the first time it had ever been brung about by a beautiful woman, and Bunny Wigglesworth was as beautiful as they come, especially when you compared her to all the other women who lived in Cougar Claw. He knew he shouldn't approach her in his chaps and buckskin shirt, and dust rising off him with every step he took, and smelling more like a horse than his horse did, but he was just so taken by her that he couldn't help himself. There were a couple of scraggly-looking flowers growing behind a water trough, and he picked 'em up, walked over to her, bowed low like he figured knights of old and maybe

Boston gentlemen did, and offered her the flowers. He thought it was kind of strange that she took them and began chewing on 'em after she thanked him, but it was charmingly strange (and probably all the rage back East), and pretty soon Jack, who sometimes went days without saying more then a couple of words, was pouring out his heart to her and begging her not to go out to Californy just yet.

He told her that he loved her with a mad undying passion, and that he just had to see her again. She explained that she was traveling with her maiden aunt, who was a teetotaler and such a stickler for early-to-bed-and-early-to-rise that her being a maiden was even less surprising than her being an aunt, and that her aunt was dead certain all men were out for just One Thing, or maybe Six Things, which at least showed that what she lacked in experience she made up for in imagination.

But her maiden aunt had been so strict, and her finishing school (whatever that was) so cloistered that, strange as it seems, Howlin' Jack was the very first man she had ever spoken to, except for some exceptionally dull uncles (and one who wasn't dull at all, but was currently serving time in Carson City for sins that didn't have no names west of Manhattan, where they were viewed more as a series of popular parlor games than a bunch of crimes against God and Nature.) And she allowed that she had plumb lost her heart to him, and promised to sneak out of the hotel as soon as her maiden aunt went to bed, and meet Jack on the outskirts of town — not a difficult feat, since town was only one block long — and maybe even steal a forbidden kiss (or perhaps six forbidden kisses, since she wasn't anywhere near as imaginative as her maiden aunt).

So they went their separate ways, each counting the minutes until they met again. (Well, actually, Jack didn't have much schooling, so he could only count the hours. Up to ten, anyway.) Then, after Bunny and her maiden aunt had gone to bed, each in their own rooms, Bunny waited until she heard the gentle snores of the older woman, quickly got out of her nightgown, climbed into her very best outfit, tiptoed out of the room and down the stairs, made her way all 85 feet to the edge of town, and a minute later was in Jack's strong, masculine arms.

"I love you, Bunny Wigglesworth," he said, "and I want you to be mine."

"And I love you, Howlin' Jack Dawkins," she said, "and I pledge to be yours forever."

"We will be so happy together, Bunny," he said. And then: "Bunny. That's a curious name. I don't think I've ever met anyone called Bunny. Not that it isn't adorable," he added quickly.

"Well, come to think of it, I've never met anyone called Howlin' Jack before," she replied. "Or even Howlin' Bill, for that matter. Why do they call you that, Jack?"

He had just opened his mouth to answer her when the sun, which had been making its lazy way to the horizon, finally vanished and night fell.

And suddenly he wasn't Howlin' Jack the cowboy any more, but instead was a large red-brown animal with a long muzzle and sharp canines. His answer came out as a howl. Then he cleared his throat and said, "Now you know my deep, dark, shameful secret. I'm a werecoyote.

"Oh my goodness!" said a high-pitched, squeaky, terrified little voice coming from somewhere around Jack's ankle. He looked down and saw a cute, furry blonde rabbit staring at him. "Now you know my secret too."

"You're a wererabbit?" said Jack, trying to sort out his feelings.

"Only at nights," said Bunny. "And please stop drooling on me. I'm getting drenched." She looked up at him. "I hope a little thing like this isn't going to come between us."

"I still love you," said Jack.

"And you don't mind the way I look?" she asked.

"You look . . . delicious," he said.

"You've changed," said Bunny accusingly.

"Of course I've changed," said Jack. "I'm a coyote. And you're a rabbit. A lovely rabbit. A delicious soft plump blonde juicy rabbit."

"You're drooling again," said Bunny.

She hopped back a step — well, a jump, actually — and he tensed.

"Don't do that!" said Jack.

"Don't do what?" she asked.

"Don't make sudden motions," he said. "I have this urge to chase little things that move fast." He stared at her with a curious expression on his coyote face. "The problem is, I have this urge to eat little things that don't move fast enough."

"Oh, cruel unfeeling Fate!" she cried. "To find you, only to lose you so soon!"

Suddenly Jack howled again. "You ain't losing me, kid!"

"I thought I was a love object, not an appetizer," said Bunny miserably.

"Why limit yourself?" growled Jack, pulling his lips back and exposing his fangs. "You can be both!"

Bunny had time for one little scream, and then she took off like a bat out of hell, or perhaps a rabbit out of finishing school, with Jack in hot pursuit. They ran due West, straight out of Cougar Claw and straight into legend.

Every now and then word comes back about a soft-spoken feller with sad, haunted eyes traveling from town to town looking for a girl with golden tresses named Bunny — and when cowboys sit around the campfire at night telling their sad stories, they always stop when they hear a coyote's mournful wail, because they know it's Howlin' Jack Dawkins, still searching for his lost love.

THE RIDER OF THE DARK

by Darrell Schweitzer

illustrated by Allen Koszowski

I see by your outfit,
that you are a cowboy.
— "The Streets of Laredo"

I met him in a steakhouse in Denver in 1927 while waiting for a train, on my way home from college at Christmas break.

He slammed a silver dollar on the counter and said, "Give me a whiskey!"

As this was a steakhouse, and Prohibition was in effect, the man behind the counter could only gape and fumble with a towel and try to explain that they didn't serve alcohol on the premises.

"When I say I want a whiskey, I want a whiskey!"

I could see that this guy was what you'd call a "character." He was old, maybe seventy, a little hunched over,

his face like old, gnarled tree-bark, his beard a bristly white. His clothes were an unsavory mix of leather and denim so worn it was shiny. Quite out of fashion.

As I drew closer, I noticed that he didn't smell too nice either.

"A whiskey!"

"Sir," said the cook behind the counter, "If you don't quiet down I shall have to call —"

Nevertheless, my instincts were aroused. Here was source material, a *story*.

The old man looked at me, hard, then his look softened when I opened my jacket and showed him the silver flask in my inside pocket. Though a freshman, I had begun to move in sophisticated circles.

"It's all right," I said to the man behind the counter. "My grandfather is here to meet me. It's okay."

We sat down. I ordered steaks for both of us. The old man snatched the flask out of my hand before I could offer it to him.

"The name's Rufus T. Harris, and I ain't your grandpappy —"

"I know, but I had to tell him something. You were making a *scene,* Mr. Harris."

He took a long swig from my flask.

"Don't I have the right to? I can't find a decent saloon in this here town —"

"It's called the 18th Amendment to the Constitution, Sir —"

"Well, *my* constitution needs a good snort now an' then —" He drank some more. "Damn, boy, that's good hootch you got there! You shouldn't be drinkin' such stuff till you got whiskers on your chin, though surely this'll raise hair if anything will, uh —"

"Yes. Is there a problem?"

"You got a name, don't you, boy?"

"Oh," I stood up and extended my

hand. "I'm so sorry. I have been impolite. My name's Blake, Robert Blake —"

He didn't take my hand, but finished my liquor and dropped the flask to the table-top, then belched. I sat down again.

"I got you pegged, Bobby Blake. You're one of them writer fellows, ain't you, wantin' to meet a real older-timer who can tell you what it's like livin' life in the raw, back when the West was really wild? Ain't that so?"

"Kind of . . ." This was not the time to explain that I really wanted to be the successor to Poe and Baudelaire, rather than Jack London. "I *am* a journalism student," I hastily added.

"Well, ain't that grand? So here's your story, Bobby Blake. No! Put that stupid notebook away! If it ain't worth rememberin' it ain't worth hearin.'"

Just then our steaks arrived. As we chowed down, he began to tell me his story.

"It was a long time ago," he said, pointing at me with his fork. "I was about your age, which means I was so wet behind the ears I didn't know a longhair from a longhorn, but I was like you in a way, Bobby Blake. I wanted to experience the whole big, wide world. I wanted manly adventure, just like in the dime novels."

The first rule of journalism, even if you're not really intending to be a journalist, is knowing when to say nothing. Don't argue. Let him think what he wanted of me. Let him get on with his tale.

"So I joined a cattle drive, back in the old days, when the railroads only came to Kansas City, and we had to drive the cattle north. My uncle Joshua convinced the trail boss, one Samuel Quintus Knight — now you remember that name, Bobby Blake, because Big Sam Q. Knight was the biggest, bravest, toughest cowboy there ever was. Why, the other cowboys told me he once shot the tip off the crescent moon with his six-shooter, and he split a man's skull

at fifty paces by spittin' a chaw of tobacco —"

He waited to see if I would react. I didn't. I just let him think I believed every word he said.

He went on with his story.

Yep, [Harris said] I was just like you, Bobby, I was. I looked up to that man like he was God. I thought he could catch the lightnin' in his bare hands. He was everything I ever wanted to be. I was terrible, terrible grateful to Uncle Josh for getting me this job, and I stuck real close to Sam Knight, because I wanted to learn everything I could from him, and I wanted him to know I'd learned everything I could *from him.* So I worked mighty hard. And, I tell you, it was the thrill of my life to be ridin' and ropin' beside him, and to sit near him around the campfire at night when he an' the boys would get out the harmonicas and guitars and make soft music to keep the cattle quiet.

I suppose that's how I come to notice the signs, then. I mean, there was something in the way Big Sam looked out into the darkness, how he watched a cloud pass over the moon and then turned his eyes away suddenly, how he made strange emblems like five-pointed stars in the sand around the edge of the camp each night, and muttered something I couldn't make out. And one night his voice faltered as he strummed a guitar and sang, *"Git along little shoggoth, it's your misfortune and none of my own."*

Almost asleep, I rolled over in my sleeping bag and asked, "What's a shoggoth, Sam?"

He stopped playing. "You don't want to know, son," was all he said. "You just don't want to know."

And that morning two men were missing, the tall cowboy named Shorty and the right-handed one named Lefty. Their horses was still there, but no sign of them. There was nothing we could do.

I could tell Big Sam had somethin' on his mind. The way he looked up at them vultures circling. The time, in broad daylight, something *dark* and huge that the eye couldn't quite wrap itself around blotted out the sun for several minutes. There weren't no Injun smoke signals atop the mesas. Nothing like that. It was quiet, too quiet, all the way, and if I knew, what more must Sam be knowing, that's what I wanted to know.

Bad signs. Of course it was the place for it. We'd passed through the Superstition River Valley, near Hanged Man's Gulch, betwixt the Screamin' Skulls Mountains, just past Great Old Ones Canyon — and you don't have to know precisely where any of those places is. Let's say west of the Pecos and North of the Rio Grande.

That's enough. Bad place. Not where you want to be caught at nightfall with ten thousand head of cattle, but night falls when it does, and there we was.

I had a bad feeling about this.

But we made camp, there in the dark. There wasn't no moon that night, and not because Big Sam had shot it neither. Just no moon, and precious few stars, though it wasn't cloudy *exactly*. There was just somethin' funny about the air, like the air itself was *thicker* than usual and you couldn't see much farther than you could spit. Not countin' that Big Sam had once kilt a man with a chaw at fifty paces — no I mean as far as any other ordinary feller could spit.

Nobody felt like singin' much that night, though the cattle was mighty restless.

So we was sittin' in the dark, just a-waitin' for something, for the sun to come up we hoped, but for something real bad to happen, we was all afraid — then something real bad happened.

There was a man a hollerin' out there in the dark somewhere. That's a real bad thing on a cattle drive, because the herd was already nervous, and any-thing that starts a stampede can get us all kilt real fast.

"Help me, fellas! Help me!"

We all got up. We reached for our guns. Somebody lit a lantern and shined it out into the darkness, where the cattle's eyes seemed to shine back at us like the eyes of wolves. It weren't natural. It was another sign. It was wrong. Now, sudden-like, the herd was quiet, too quiet, and then there came staggering into the firelight none other than Tex Weinstein, the scruffiest, mangiest owlhoot in the outfit, with a beard like a tumbleweed and a little cloud of horseflies that seemed to follow him everywhere. But he'd always been good enough at cowboy work, even though he was just a bit of a moron, who would sometimes talk gibberish and just stare at you and say "I don't know how" till you whapped him on the head with the handle of your six-shooter to snap him out of it . . . but that wasn't gonna do no good now because, we couldn't help but notice as he come moseyin' into the firelight, his eyes was all rolled till only the whites showed, and the top of his head was chawed clean off.

He spoke in a weird, gurgly voice. "It's too late. You didn't help me."

Big Sam just drawed out his pearl-handled six-shooter and plugged Weinstein right through both of them blank eyes. *But he kept on comin'!* I tell you, it was the most god-awful thing I ever seen in my life. Sam shot him again and it took off most of his head, till there was just his jaws a'flappin' and slobberin.' *But he kept on comin'!*

So we all backed away as he came into the firelight, his hands out to grab us like they was claws, black ooze sputterin' from out of where his brain used to be.

Real quick Sam drawned one of them five-pointed signs in the dust — *sigils* he called 'em — and when Tex Weinstein stepped in that he was caught somehow, and just blundered around, gropin' at the air, and Sam shot him one more time through the heart and he dropped down to the ground, stone dead.

Only it was obvious he'd been dead all along, living dead. I got out my own gun, just to be sure he was *dead* dead. But Sam pushed the barrel aside and said, "Don't waste your ammo, Rufus. You're gonna need it."

I looked down at the *dead* dead man who seemed content to stay that way.

"What happened to him, Sam?" was all I could say and what we all wanted to know.

"He be a *zombie,*" said Louisiana Louie. "I seen things like that down in the swamps outside New Orleans. Them black folks can raise up a dead man like that with their African magic —"

"It wasn't African magic," said Big Sam, holsterin' his pistol. "It was a whole lot worse." And he told us then, what nobody could believe if they hadn't seen it and what nobody could forget in all their born days if they had, how we just happened to be, at the worst time of the year in the worst place, because Great Old Ones Canyon wasn't called that fer nothin'. *Millions* and *millions* of years ago the Old Ones, monsters or devils or something, come down from the stars on a dark night like this, when there wasn't no moon and the darkness was, *thicker* somehow, like the air opened up and there was something even darker behind it. And these Old Ones was sleepin' in that canyon, waitin' for something like Judgment Day, when they could come up out of the ground and take over the whole world. But meantime, when the stars was *just right,* they could sometimes walk through the desert night in dreams — I didn't quite know what that meant, but that's what Big Sam said — and if you ran into a dream-ghost of a Great Old One, and you happened to be dead, that would turn you into a zombie, it stood to reason.

"But it *don't* stand to reason," I said, amazed and terrified that I would actually say something against the trail boss at a time like this, but it didn't, and I said so. "It *don't* stand to no reason because Tex *wasn't dead.* I mean sometimes with him, when he gets funny, maybe you ain't so sure, but he ate his grub tonight, so I *don't think* he was dead —"

"The boy's right," said Coyote Jim the Halfbreed. "He wasn't dead, so he musta got turned into a zombie some other way."

"There is only one way," said Louisiana Louie. "For a living man to get turned into a zombie, he has to get bit by a zombie."

Some of the other cowboys joined in.

"That's why the top of his head was chawed off then?"

"Stands to reason."

It took them a while to work out the implications.

"That means there's *another zombie out there!*"

"Among the herd!"

"My God! We gotta protect the herd!"

Now what I wanted to know, and didn't have time to ask about, was why the whole top of Tex Weinstein's head was chawed off, because, well, a man's mouth ain't big enough to take a bite like that.

Just then a strange and eerie *mooing* came out of the darkness, like a long, lonesome wind, but with a voice, saying things you'd rather not hear.

I didn't have time to ask anything more because Big Sam shined the lantern out at the herd again, and we saw that every last one of them longhorn steers had its eyes rolled up all white, and them white eyes was *glowin'* like a million evil stars.

"It's too late to save the cattle," Big Sam said.

All of a sudden Louisiana Louie let out a shriek, because a zombie-eyed steer had lunged out of the darkness and caught his head in its foaming mouth. He wriggled a bit, but it wasn't no use. The critter chawed off the top of his skull and sucked out his brain as we watched. Then he came at us, hands out like claws, all a'slobberin' and most of us together shot out his eyes — which distracted him long enough for big Sam to make another of them *sigils* in the sand. When Louie — or what used to be Louie — stepped into it, we plugged him in the heart and that was the end of him.

"How did you learn to do that?" I asked Sam, pointing at the *sigil*.

"When you're trail boss long enough, son," he said, "you learn all sorts of things that come in handy."

Again, my heart swelled up with sheer hero-worship. "Jeepers —"

But there was no time for that.

All of us high-tailed it after that. We couldn't even get to our horses, because we heard the horses screamin' and we knowed that the cattle got to them first. It ain't a smart idea to ride a zombie horse. So we ran on foot, the cattle closin' in, until we reached the base of a rocky hill.

There we made our stand, shootin' out the eyes of the zombie longhorns, which continued to distract them a mite, but didn't kill them.

And among the rocks, there was no place to draw a *sigil*.

And we was runnin' out of bullets.

Up we climbed, up, and up, the cattle comin' after us. Somehow a dead steer can climb a lot better'n a live one. Don't ask me why. Maybe it's just more determined to catch up with a living man and chaw out his brain.

Another scream, and one of 'em got Coyote Jim the Halfbreed.

Up. There wasn't much of any place to go.

Fortunately we came to an open, sandy spot, where Big Sam could make another *sigil*, so we was able to plug what used to be the Halfbreed and a dozen of the cattle, but there was too many of 'em, and our ammo, and our numbers was runnin' out, as the zom-

bie cattle zombified one more cowboy after another.

At last it was only me and Big Sam at the top of the hill, back to back. I can tell you I was scairt. Who wouldn't be? As far as we could see, in every direction, zombie longhorns with eyes like glowing coals was coming at us, up, up to chaw out our brains.

But that wasn't the worst of it. Maybe I was plumb crazy already, but I swear as I looked up into the sky, I seen *behind* what few stars there were, enormous shapes, faces, the dreaming ghosts of the Great Old Ones walking above Great Old One Canyon, and some of them had faces full of feelers like squids, and some had wings, and burning eyes, and none of them was like anything you ever seen on Earth; and I knew that they *hated* us more than words could express, and were just lookin' for the chance to wipe us all out like some goddamn vermin they think we are.

I had only one bullet left. I put the muzzle of my gun under my chin and said, "Well, Sam, I wanted to grow up to be just like you, 'cause you're my hero, but I guess I ain't gonna get the chance." I was sobbin' then, I am not ashamed to say.

But Sam he took the gun away from my chin and he said, gently, like a daddy would to his boy, "There is another way, Rufus. But only for one of us." He pressed what felt like a piece of smooth, cold stone into my hand. "This is something else I picked up 'cause it might come in handy someday. It's called a shining trapezohedron. Stare into it like you is looking far, far away. You'll see something movin' in there. Call it to you. Ask it for help. There will be a price you have to pay. But it is the only way. Do it. Now give me your gun, and I'll try to distract them a bit more so you have a chance."

He took my gun, and put his last six bullets into his own, yelled "Yippie ki-yi-yo!" and charged down into the zombie herd, blastin' away. I don't think he got very far.

Then it was up to me. I held the shining trapezohedron in both of my hands and stared into it hard, and, yes, it was shining somehow, with light of its own, and then it seemed that a million stars flowed *out* of it like water out of a geyser, and I was *falling down* but into the sky at the same time, and the wind was howlin' all around me like the worst winter blizzard you ever heard with a hundred tornados joined in as chorus, and then I was lookin' out on *someplace else,* a different world, that was like a desert of blue ice, with three or four blue suns in the sky that didn't give off no heat at all.

And I saw, ridin' across that blue desert, a man all in black, but for his *silk mask,* which was yellow, and very strange because the bulges behind it didn't suggest a *human* face at all, not like he had a nose or a chin or anything . . . but Big Sam had told me what to do, and I done it. I called out to the rider of the dark, in something other than words, because when I opened my mouth there was only more howlin' of the wind, but somehow my *thought* was sent to him, and he heard me, and he turned in his course and came ridin' right at me, closer and closer, and I thought he was gonna ride me down, but at the last minute he grabbed me up like I was a little child and swung me up behind him in the saddle, and I clung to him as he rode down the rocky hillside. He didn't use his reins. His horse didn't need guiding. He had *black,* shiny six-guns in both hands, blazing away, and even after he'd shot a thousand times, he didn't run out of bullets, and somehow when he did it, as if *he himself was the sigil,* he kilt them zombies and zombie cattle, every last one of them. We rode on for hours, blastin' away, up and down the hill, all across the plain, into Great Old One Canyon and out again, shootin' and shootin' until there was nothin' left movin' anywheres, and then the sun come up, and the masked rider seemed to just fade away like mist, and I landed on the ground with a bump, and I didn't have no six-gun (because Sam had took mine), just the shining trapezohedron in my hand, and there was thousands of dead zombie cattle and dead zombie cowboys as far as the eye could see.

Then all I could do was walk, for days and nights without stoppin', without eatin' or drinkin', until I had become completely crazed, and it was all like a terrible dream that never, never ended. And I don't think it ever did end, even when I come to a farmhouse and fell down fainted on the floor. I remember thinkin', *Who was that masked man anyway?* and I remembered answerin' myself that he'd said his name was Nigel, Nigel R. Lathotep . . . some kinda Irish name, I think. And I laughed and laughed at that like I didn't have no brain left at all, and the folks that took me in thought I was just delirious, but what did they know? They had not *seen* what I had *seen*, now, had they?

Old Rufus Harris was still laughing over the table in the steakhouse when he finished this. "Now what do ya think of my story, Bobby Blake?" he said. "What do ya think? Did I give you the *real stuff?*" And he went on cackling and wheezing and cackling some more, so much that I was acutely aware that people were beginning to stare.

"Please, Sir," I said desperately.

He paused for just a moment to gaze longingly into my empty silver flask.

"I don't suppose you got any more of this fine concoction — ?"

He started cackling again, louder and louder.

I had no choice. I got out the spare I carried in my boot. I had hoped to save that one for the holidays.

He snatched it from me and drained it.

"So, Bobby Blake, what'cha think?"

I measured my words carefully. I refrained from saying that, yes, he had given me the *real stuff,* because, having planned a career of writing about grotesquerie, horror, and the insane, it was helpful to make the acquaintance of a genuine, raving lunatic.

Instead I merely asked him about the *price* Big Sam had mentioned.

"Oh, that," he said. He got out what looked like a shiny black stone, perhaps a piece of obsidian, cut strangely, with many angles, so the eye could not quite grasp its shape. It was, of course the shining trapezohedron. He began to explain, in a voice that faded away as the wind roared louder and louder, how he had exchanged death for deathless bondage, how he was now an eternal servant of the Rider of the Dark, whose name was, more properly *Nyarlathotep,* and it was his task to recruit more such slaves like himself, whether willing or unwilling, it did not matter. "Ain't no use fightin', boy," he said. "You can't get away nohow."

Then I heard nothing more, and, staring into the shining trapezohedron, I seemed to be falling *down* into the starry sky, and gazing, or floating, over the frigid blue desert beneath the cold blue suns, as the rider in the silken mask drew ever closer to me.

It was only with the greatest strength of will that I broke away. I pushed the black stone back at the old man, then ran screaming from the room, out into the street and across to the train station, where, I discovered, I had missed my train.

Then I fell down faint, into a delirium, and I heard a voice whispering in my mind, the voice which inspires all my nightmare visions, all the hideous and terrible and strangely beautiful writings for which I have since become famous.

We shall meet again, Robert Blake, it says. *Though you flee to the ends of the Earth, it is no distance. We shall meet again.*

TROUBLE IN CTHULHU CANYON

A Deputy Sheriff of Devil's Doorknob Novel

by Ron Goulart

illustrated by Russell Morgan

This story began in the January issue.

The events leading up to this installment:

Handsome, stalwart Whistlin' Jim Destiny, Jr. was peacefully studying to be an alienist at prestigious Harvard University in the year of 1883 and was looking forward to the next semester when he was due to find out what an alienist was. But then a fateful telegram arrived from the Far West, informing him that his beloved, crusty old father, Whistlin' Jim Destiny, Sr., had disappeared under mysterious circumstances.

The elder Destiny was sheriff in the wide-open Montana town of Devil's Doorknob and was known as "the fastest gun West of the Pecos, North of East Moline, and Southwest of Dayton." Young Jim immediately boarded a train for the Far West and the wide-open Devil's Doorknob.

En route he meets fellow passenger Maribelle Van Horn, a pale and lovely blonde who is going to Devil's Doorknob to become the schoolmarm. She is somewhat uneasy, because she's heard that the previous three schoolmarms were tarred and feathered and run out of town on rails. She confesses to Jim that feathers make her sneeze.

When the train is still a day from its destination, the conductor confides in Jim, since he's the only man aboard with an honest face, that he's worried about most of the recent passengers. They include the James Boys, the Younger Brothers, the Wild Bunch, the Daltons, and Dockstader's Minstrels. The railroad can't afford both a train robbery and a minstrel show all at once.

Just as the gaggle of train robbers is about to make its move, and the minstrels are tuning up their banjos, a chilling, bloodcurdling scream is heard from the direction of the baggage car ahead.

Pale, shaking in his every limb, the baggage clerk comes staggering into the coach. Trembling, he clutches at the sleeve of the plump conductor.

"What's wrong, Reisberson?" inquires the conductor.

"Inside that coffin . . ."

"Which coffin?"

"The fancy one we're supposed to deliver to the wide-open Montana town of Devil's Doorknob."

"Oh, that coffin. What about it, man?"

"I heard an . . . unearthly sound from within, sir," the shaken man manages to gasp. "When I opened it I saw . . . good lord, it's indescribable!"

"Could you at least make a try?"

"Well, it's unspeakably foul . . ."

"You're off to a good start," encourages the conductor. "Keep going."

"Beg pardon, gents," says Jesse James politely, rising up from his seat next to his brother Frank. "Did I hear yuh mention the wide-open Montana town of Devil's Doorknob?"

The shuddering baggage man gasps, "Yes, we're carrying a coffin to Devil's

by Ron Goulart												61

Doorknob from a far off European country name of Transylvania and —"

"Say no more," yelps Jesse James, letting out a horrified howl. Screaming, he and his gang go running down the aisle and jump off the moving train.

The eldest Younger Brother leaps up off his seat. "A coffin for Devil's Doorknob, did you say?"

The conductor, now pale and perspiring himself, replies, "Yep."

"Aaiee," cries the eldest Younger and goes stomping, babbling what might be prayers, along the aisle to leap from the puffing train. He is followed by the next oldest Younger Brother, the younger Younger Brothers and the youngest Younger Brother.

Soon, all the potential robbers, yowling in fear, have flung themselves free of the train.

Dockstader's Minstrels, after packing up their banjos and tambourines, follow suit. Then only the quivering baggage clerk, the stunned conductor, Maribelle Van Horn, and Whistlin' Jim, Jr. are left aboard the westbound railroad car.

The new schoolmarm sighs. "This does not bode well," she says to Jim. "It seems to me that Devil's Doorknob must have an awfully unsavory reputation."

"Nonsense," Jim says soothingly. "Why, it's no worse than any other wide-open Wild West town, miss. My old dad, until he mysteriously and inexplicably vanished, wrote me jolly letters once a month extolling the virtues of Devil's Doorknob. If one discounted the frequent gunfire, the muddy streets, the abundance of saloons and bordellos, he assured me the little place is not that much different than Boston."

"I've never thought all that much of Boston, yet I suppose —"

"Devil's Doorknob," cuts in the anguished conductor, "has got a whole lot worse, folks, since Luke Satan become mayor."

Before Jim can speak up in defense of his father's place of business, the door of the car slaps open. A gaunt man in formal attire and a scarlet-lined black cape comes shambling angrily in. He is gaunt of figure, pale as death, and he speaks English with a strong trace of an obscure European accent.

"What's the big idea of all this hollering and stomping?" he inquires angrily. "There I was, I mean to say, sleeping peacefully in my coffin when some ninny makes an unholy noise prying open the lid to gape at me. Then all sorts of rowdy behavior commences up here. Frankly, I've a mind to complain to the railroad company and . . ." He glances out the windows and grows even paler. "My goodness, it's still daylight."

The caped figure begins to moan forlornly.

"Everybody knows what sunshine does to vampires. Is this any way to run a railroad? I . . ."

As the horrified group looks on, the man swiftly turns to dust, his now empty garments falling to a sooty tangle upon the swaying floor of the rattling railroad car.

"How the heck am I going to explain this to the shipping company?" laments the baggage man.

Maribelle, sighing profoundly, faints dead away.

By the time she comes to, the remains of the mysterious vampire have been swept up, and an unnatural calm has descended upon the westbound train.

The remainder of the journey is relatively uneventful. But when they are about an hour away from Devil's Doorknob, the afternoon suddenly turns dark as night. Soon torrential rains are pounding at the swaying train cars. Lightning crackles all around, thunder roars.

"That is one other unpleasant thing that my father mentioned about the town," Whistlin' Jim informs the pretty schoolmarm. "The weather is frequently inclement."

When they arrive at Devil's Doorknob, Whistlin' Jim and Maribelle find that the mayor is there to welcome them.

"Howdy, folks," greets Mayor Luke Satan. "Right glad you made it safely. I surely hope the octopuses didn't bother you?"

"Octopi?" inquires the schoolmarm, clinging to Jim's arm.

"This darn rainy weather does seem to bring them out, miss," explains the mayor. "Sometimes they even like to loll around on the railroad tracks."

"We saw nary an octopus," Jim assures him. "Might I ask, by the bye, why you're wearing that long white robe and golden crown, Mr. Mayor?"

"Shucks, that's an easy one. I'm a druid," replies Luke Satan. "In this part of Montana, the Druid Party's right popular. Now if you'll excuse me for a minute, I'll fetch that coffin I been expecting."

A brief argument between the mayor and the baggage clerk ensues. After invoking several elder gods, Mayor Satan reluctantly agrees to accept the coffin, even though it's no longer full. He then escorts Whistlin' Jim and Maribelle into town.

"Now, I got to tell you right off," he says as their buggy reaches the main street, "that this storm that just now ended blew the school house clean away, Miss Van Horn. But don't you fret none, cause I've arranged for you to teach the younguns in our least successful house of ill repute. They got lots of spare room."

"A house of ill repute?" gasps the startled girl, holding tighter to Jim's arm.

"Hereabouts the place is known as the Shunned Bordello, but don't let that worry you none. There ain't been any strange doings there for might nigh a year," explains the mayor. "And we got rid of all the rats in the walls."

Devil's Doorknob seems to consist of two square blocks of low ramshackle buildings. The dirt streets are muddy and, although it's hardly four o'clock in the afternoon, there is a feeling of grim twilight.

The sheriff's office is housed in a small adobe building that sits between the Stonehenge Saloon and the Cloven Hoof Blacksmith Shop.

After dropping the reluctant Maribelle off at the Shunned Bordello, Mayor Satan takes Jim to his missing father's office. "Let me ask you, son," the white-robed mayor says as he hitches the horses to the railing, "how you feel about strange rites."

"Neutral, I guess."

Nodding, the mayor asks, "And ancient sorceries?"

"I haven't though much about the subject," he admits. "Actually I rushed out here from Boston to find out what's become of my missing father, sir."

"How'd you like to take his place for a while? Be the Deputy Sheriff of Devil's Doorknob?"

"I don't know. I —"

"As deputy sheriff, my boy, you could restore law and order to Devil's Doorknob and hunt around for your daddy."

"I suppose I could handle the job temporarily."

"That's swell. And your office is just a hoot and a holler from the Shunned Bordello." Mayor Satan unlocks the oaken door of the office. "I could tell right off that our new schoolmarm is sweet on you."

"All right, I'll take the position. Now what can you tell me about my father?"

"Well, he just up and vanished." The mayor pushes the door open and invites Whistlin' Jim inside.

The shadowy office is damp, smelling faintly of ancient seaweed. There is a general feeling of foreboding about all the furniture.

"Up and vanished?"

"Disappeared. Just like that!" Because of the damp, the mayor's attempt to snap his fingers fails.

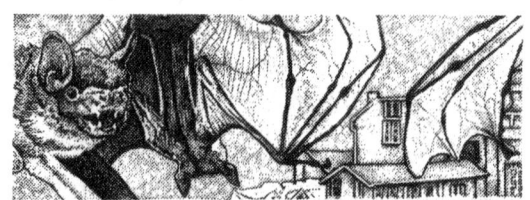

"Where did it happen?"

"Just outside of town, son, on the road to the Lazy Pentagram Ranch," explains the mayor, seating himself behind the sheriff's sturdy, but warped, desk. "See, Sheriff Destiny was riding out to talk to old man Carter about his rustling problem."

"Cattle rustling?"

The mayor coughs into his fist. "Well, not exactly cattle."

"Did this rancher see my dad?"

"Nope, old Randy Carter didn't see your pappy at all. All he seen was the bats — and them only from a distance."

Sitting down in the room's only other chair, Jim asks, "Bats?"

"Gigantic bats I guess you might call them. Carter seen a spec on the horizon, which he's pretty dang sure was your daddy. Then he seen a flock of about six or seven of these big old bats come swooping down. Next time he looked there wasn't nobody in the saddle no more."

"When you say gigantic — how big?"

"Old man Carter says about the size of his prize bull."

"That is big."

"Specially for a bat."

"You think my father was carried off by these large bats?"

"That was sure what Carter thought. I rode out that way once we realized your pappy was missing, looked all around," continues the mayor, taking a cigar out of a desk drawer and lighting it. "Found his horse, Leonard, and —"

"My father rode a horse named Leonard?"

"My the time he bought him from Derleth's Stables, all the really good horse names was gone, son — you know, like Silver, Thunder, Tony, Seabiscuit."

He exhales smoke. "I took some townspeople and we searched all over, even in the caves near Cthulhu Canyon. Never found nothing."

"What do you think happened to my father, Mayor?"

Satan shrugs. "Beats me, son," he answers. "Now, Devil's Doorknob ain't the most law-abiding town hereabouts and naturally your daddy made his share of enemies. Why even our local preacher didn't much like him. That was mostly because of the stand your father took on human sacrifice, but —"

"I'd like to start my job as deputy sheriff tomorrow, sir. Meantime, where can I reside?"

"I was so certain you was going to take this job, Jimmy, that I reserved you a suite at the Hotel Miskatonic," the mayor tells him. "You'll find it real comfortable, but you may have to give it up now and then because that's where a couple of our churches hold their wakes. You're not especially bothered by corpses, are you?"

"I don't believe so, but —"

"Good. That's a good quality in a deputy sheriff."

Over the next few days Whistlin' Jim works at being a good deputy. He is surprised to find that there is little or no activity in Devil's Doorknob by day. When night falls, the little town comes to life and the activity at the numerous saloons, bordellos, and gambling joints commences.

He asks a lot of questions about his missing father, but finds out little. In fact, most of the citizens, though they profess to have liked Whistlin' Jim Destiny, Sr., seem very reluctant, if not outright afraid to talk about him and his possible fate.

Maribelle and Jim become increasingly good friends. She is very uneasy about her teaching chores, though. There are only three pupils in her school, all large pasty-faced louts in their late teens who smell strongly of the sea at low tide. Since there is no ocean anywhere near Montana, this strikes Maribelle as an unsettling anomaly.

One rare sunny morning, soon after Jim has opened his office for the day and strapped on the gunbelt that Mayor Satan has loaned him, the lovely schoolmarm comes rushing breathlessly in.

"Jim dear," she gasps, "I'm terribly frightened."

"More so than yesterday, darling?" he asks as he settles her into a chair and takes hold of her dainty hand.

After considering his query, the schoolmarm replies, "I'd say about 40 to 50% more terrified."

"Have those louts been pulling pranks in the classroom again? That business with the dead goat was —"

"I received a shipment of school books today."

"From whom, dear?"

"That's just it, darling — I have no idea. When I arrived in the class room this morning, there was a wooden carton of books sitting on one of the loveseats. And all three of my strange, loutish pupils were already there, snickering in a most chilling way."

"Was there a bill of lading? Perhaps that will give us a clue as to —"

"There was only this note, scrawled in a crabbed hand on a piece of bloody-splattered butcher paper, dear."

Taking the wrinkled missive, Whistlin' Jim read it aloud. " 'You better start teaching from these here books, little missy! Lest you meet the grim fate of your three predecessors!' Unsigned."

"Yes, and the books . . ." She sighs. "They are vile."

"What are the titles of these supposed text books, dear?"

Maribelle takes a deep breath. "What was in that unspeakable crate was six copies of something called McGuffey's Necronomicon."

"Seems to me I saw that title on a list of Forbidden Books that they keep locked deep down in the basement of the Harvard Library."

"Be that as it may, dear," says the distraught girl, "I shall not teach from such a book." She sighs yet again. "But I don't want to lose my new job."

"Or be tarred and feathered."

"That, too."

"I reckon, as they say hereabouts, Maribelle, that I better escort you back to that school room," Whistlin' Jim offers.

"After that I'm going to have a talk with the School Board."

"You can't do that right now," she reminds him. "They sleep all day and only come out after the sun sets."

"That's right, dear, thanks for reminding me. I'll see them once darkness settles on Devil's Doorknob."

"I will feel a lot safer, Jim, with you escorting me to —"

Just then the door is shoved open and a grizzled desert rat comes rushing breathlessly in. It's T. Tumbleweed Thompson, who's acting as Jim's assistant.

Yanking off his bedraggled Stetson, Tumbleweed says, "Tarnation, Jimmy, you better hightail it over to Cthulhu Canyon right quick."

"What's the matter?"

"A bunch of them mystical devotees are fixin' to sacrifice your pappy to some eldritch gods."

Chapter XIII: The Weird Shadow Over Cthulhu

Something strange and unholy had eaten part of Whistlin' Jim Destiny, Jr.'s, horse. Therefore, he had to borrow Maribelle's buggy to cover the nine miles out to the canyon. All the while he was wondering where his father had been all this time and what he'd done to annoy the mystical devotees.

He reached the canyon just as night was falling. What he saw appalled and astonished him.

This story will be concluded in our next issue.

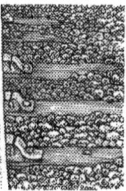

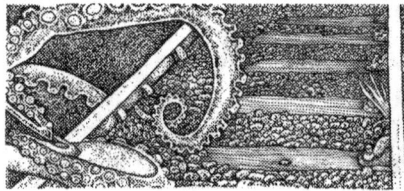

THE DEVIL'S TUNE

by & illustrated by Ray Faraday Nelson

He got off the stagecoach around sunset, tall, gaunt, and pale in a black suit and black stovepipe hat. I could see right away there was something odd about him, that he wasn't just an easterner, but some kind of European. They don't make that kind of suit in the good old USA.

No, he just didn't look right yo me, but all the same I hauled myself up from my rocking chair and ambled over to him, extending my hand. "Howdy, stranger. Welcome to Crossroads, Nevada."

He looked at my hand a moment, as if it might be dirty, then gave me a limp handshake. His hand was dry as paper and cold, real cold. "Thank you, Monsieur."

There was an awkward pause, then I said, "They call me Parson Paul. I'm the preacher man at the local church. I kind of like to meet up with folks who come to Crossroads, tell them about our church, maybe show them around. And you?"

"I am called Asmodeus. I am a concert violinist. You may have heard of me."

"Can't say as I have, Mister Asmodeus. You staying over or just passing through?"

"I had planned to continue on my way to the coast tomorrow morning, but this is such a quaint little village . . ." He looked around with a calculating eye.

"Well, sir, if you stay until Sunday, I'd be mighty happy to see you in a pew at the Crossroads Community Church. There's only the one church here, but we take in all denominations; Baptist, Methodist, Catholic, even Jewish. All men are brothers, we like to say. Yep, we all agree on ten things, them old ten commandments. Everybody agrees to that."

"Even Hindus, Buddhists, Moslems?"

"Well, we don't have no Hindus, Buddhists, or Moslems in Crossroads, so that problem don't come up. I'm sure we could work something out with any religion there is."

His thin, bloodless lips curled. "Any religion there is?"

There was another awkward pause, then I asked him, "You looking for a hotel?"

"A hotel? Yes, that would be nice."

"We only got one hotel in this town, The Last Chance Hotel. There used to be a dance hall and gambling room there on the first floor, but I got the townspeople together and shut that down. I'll show you the way."

"Oh? There used to be a dance hall?"

"That's right, mister. The stage and a lot of chairs and tables are still there gathering dust. Follow me. I'll show you. We got a boy who'll carry your luggage."

"Except for one thing I always carry myself." He reached into the stagecoach and hauled out a black violin case. As I crossed the dirt street, he followed me, hugging that fiddle case to his chest like it was his baby son. Tom, the fetch and carry boy, tagged along with the maestro's steamer trunk on a hand truck.

We got the Great Man's autograph on the guest book, then he wandered into the abandoned dance hall and stood a long time, deep in thought. There was something about the darkened room that gave me the creeps, but it didn't seem to bother this gent. I piped up, "Well, I guess I'll be on my way. If you need anything . . ."

He turned his gaze on me. "Ah, Parson Paul, I think I will be staying over for quite a while. You and I, we will become good friends, no?"

He took my hand in his. He had the coldest hand I'd ever touched, colder than the hand of the dead men at funerals over the years that I'd given a send-off to the Promised Land.

The sun had set by the time I came out of the hotel, and after sundown here in the desert it gets really dark. I mean, you can see all the stars in Heaven like glowing clouds, but down here on Earth there's just blackness, except for an occasional lantern shining out from a window. Somebody could sneak up on you in the middle of the street and you wouldn't see him.

I pulled back my overcoat and felt for my hip holster. Yep, there was my faithful Colt 45 revolver, ready for action. They don't call me Paul, the Pistol Packing Parson for nothing. I ain't never killed nobody, but there's been times I had to take my trusty Colt out and lay it on the pulpit to get a little respect.

One of those lanterns, down at the far end of the street, was in the window of the parsonage, and I knew my wife Faith was waiting there for me with a delicious hot meal. I walked faster, almost tripping over a watering trough. It you want to know the truth, I was scared. Scared of what? Bless my soul, I hadn't the faintest notion.

I actually broke into a run the last block, and when I stomped up the front steps and across the porch, I was panting like a hound dog.

I burst in and slammed the door behind me, then I bolted it. You know, I hadn't felt I had to bolt that door since the dance hall shut down.

Faith was frowning as she came out of the kitchen, wiping her hands on her apron. Lord help me, even in an apron with no makeup or anything, she sure was the prettiest woman in Crossroads.

"What's eating you, Paul?" she asked curtly. "You look like you seen a ghost."

I hugged her tight and gave her a long kiss. When I finally let her go she laughed and said, "If there is a ghost out there, invite him in. I'd like to give him a vote of thanks for that kiss."

"No ghost." I went into the kitchen and sat down at the table.

She followed me in. "What then?"

"Nothing. Nothing at all."

She set a steaming bowl of stew on the table and sat down across from me. We bowed our heads and I said grace, then we ate a while in silence.

We were almost done when she spoke again. "Surely there was something that upset you. You can tell me, Honey." She rested her hand on my arm.

by & illustrated by Ray Faraday Nelson

"A stranger came into town on the stagecoach."

"A gambler? A gun slinger?"

"Nothing like that. A concert violinist."

"Well, bless my soul, what is there about a concert violinist that could throw the fear of God into you?"

"I don't rightly know. He don't look . . . He don't look quite human."

"Not quite human? Come on, now. This town could use a concert violinist. Lord knows we don't see much culture around here. When I was growing up back east, my daddy took me to concerts all the time. I got to know what real music sounds like."

"Oh? Maybe you should have married someone else, someone more cultured."

"Now don't carry on like that, Honey. That stranger, he's only passing through?"

"He said he might stay a while."

"Then you ask him to come and play his violin in our church."

I jumped to my feet. "Never! That man ain't never going to play his damn fiddle in my church!"

"My stars! Now don't get all stirred up over nothing. I sware I never saw the like! If you don't want him playing in your church, then he won't play there. Only maybe the board of trustees might take a different view."

"You'd go over my head to the board of trustees?"

"Now never you mind. I won't do no such a thing. Only I thought this is supposed to be a community church. The trustees ought to have a voice in things."

"Not in this matter!" I found I could hardly speak.

"All right, all right. Calm down, Paul. You're all on edge. You get a good night's sleep and you'll see this ain't worth all that fuss."

I went to bed, but I didn't sleep much. Faith, though, she snored like a pig.

The following morning I was in my customary sunny place in my rocking chair in front of the stagecoach office when I saw Mister Asmodeus striding across the street toward me. I muttered to myself, "Uh oh," then stood up to greet him.

He gave me one of those cold handshakes of his, then said, in his deep, unsettling voice, "Parson Paul, I have good news!"

I gestured toward a vacant rocking chair next to mine. "Sit down and tell me about it."

When we were seated, he put his icy hand on my knee and announced, "I am giving a concert."

"Where?"

"In the dance hall. Saturday night. The hotel owner is all for it, and the sheriff has given his permission. One of his deputies has already volunteered to collect admissions at the door."

"Funny they didn't consult me."

"The hotel owner told me not to. He seems to still be a bit resentful about you closing his dance hall." Asmodeus chuckled. "I think he sees my concert as a way of getting back at you."

This was the first I'd heard about anyone carrying a grudge against me for doing the Lord's work. I said, "I see."

Asmodeus leaned closer. "But don't worry. I am your friend. I will not do the concert if you don't want me to."

It took me a while to answer. "Go ahead. Do the concert."

"Thank you! I needed your blessing!"

A shadow fell over us and I looked up. There stood my wife, Faith, looming over us.

She was wearing her best dress, the one she ordinarily only wore in church, all blue with white lace decorations, and she was carrying her new blue parasol.

"Paul darling," she said. "Won't you introduce me to your friend?"

Asmodeus and I stood up. I said, "Faith, this is Mister Asmodeus that I told you about. Mister Asmodeus, this is my wife, Faith."

He bowed. She curtsied.

He said, "I am surprised to find such beauty here on the frontier. A woman like you would grace the salons of Paris."

"Thank you, kind sir. We women are like soldiers. We pretty much go where we're sent."

We sat down, I on her right, he on her left.

She said, "I saw a poster at the hotel. You're giving a concert?"

"Oh yes, Madam, since your husband has been so kind as to give the project his blessing."

She glanced at me with surprise. "You gave it your blessing?"

"I couldn't say no." I forced a smile.

"Wonderful!" She clapped her hands together, then turned away from me. "Monsieur, what pieces do you plan to play?"

"The usual classics, for the most part. The one exception will be an ancient folk song I have collected in my travels. Nobody knows how old it is, but it was certainly being played all over Europe long before the birth of Christ. There are words to it, but I won't sing them. They're in a language so long forgotten nobody can identify it, let alone translate it."

"Fascinating!" she exclaimed. "Any idea what kind of song it might be?"

"Most likely it is a kind of hymn."

"A hymn?" I said. "Before the birth of Christ?"

"Oh yes."

Faith chimed in brightly, "But it doesn't matter, does it, since we'll only hear the tune, not the words."

"All the same, " I said, "can't we skip that piece?"

Asmodeus threw up his hands. "But no! It is the climax of the whole performance! It never fails to bring down the house!"

Faith pleaded, "Don't spoil the concert, Paul. My goodness, can't you bend a teeny tiny bit?"

"Very well, very well," I grumbled.

"Have it your own way. What do I know about culture anyway?"

"That's a good boy." She patted me on the arm.

I had the strongest feeling that her hand was cold, like the hand of Mister Asmodeus, but no, that was impossible.

Saturday seemed to come at me like a runaway locomotive, and there was no way I could get off the tracks. A blur of tense days and sleepless nights, and I was there, sweating in the oppressive late afternoon heat in a line of Crossroads citizens in their Sunday best outside the entrance to the dance hall. Faith stood beside me, eyes glistening with an excitement I had not seen since our wedding day.

The years had fallen away from her, revealing a young bride headed for the altar, unaware of the hardships and loneliness that lay ahead of her, of the price she would have to pay for being a preacher's wife.

My whole congregation was there, even those families who had stopped coming to church after my crusade against the dance hall, even those contrary souls who never set foot in my chapel unless someone had died, been born or was getting married. I couldn't help but wonder what this stranger with his damn fiddle had to offer that didn't. The worst of it was Frank Armitage's wife Margie, who had always played the pedal organ at my services and who would now play the piano accompaniments for the Great Asmodeus.

Through the wide front windows of the dance hall I could see lanterns being lit along the edge of the stage. Soon the whole room in there would be in darkness except for the yellow glow around the battered upright piano, focussing all attention on the two musicians. There was something romantic, something magical about that lighting. Maybe people would come to church more if I held my services in the evening by lantern light.

The line began to move. There was a rustle as people took out their money, a muted jingle of coins. Faith squeezed my hand and whispered, "Isn't it wonderful?"

When I reached the door the deputy who was collecting the money held up his hand and said, "You and your wife get in free, Parson Paul. The maestro has reserved seats for you both in the front row."

Another deputy, acting as an usher, led us to our place, the best seats in the house.

After we were settled in, Faith whispered, "Wasn't that sweet of him?"

Behind us the murmur of excited voices was like the sound of crickets in the evening back east, where I'd grown up. There were no crickets in Crossroads, and no fireflies. Bugs have more sense than to come to a place like this.

Nobody acted like this while waiting for my sermons. Heck, I was lucky if they didn't snore too loud while I was preaching.

The crowd quieted down. Somebody closed the front doors. It was so quiet you could hear the wind moaning in the eaves like a woman in ecstasy.

Then he appeared, in black tie and tails, the star, the master, the focus of all attention, Monsieur Asmodeus. He entered from stage left, violin in hand, stepping quickly into the central circle of light, and took a bow. The accompanist followed, sheet music clutched to her bosom, the rims of her spectacles gleaming intermittently with reflections from the lanterns.

The crowd exploded with applause. My God, he was getting a standing ovation before he had played a note!

The applause faded.

He spoke.

"Monsieurs and Mesdames, welcome to the first of what I hope will be many evenings for you and me. For some time now the lights of this stage have been snuffed out, but always remember, every sunset is followed by a sunrise. That which lives must someday die, but that which dies must always live again. In the darkest hour before dawn, that is when the birds begin to sing, welcoming the new day. Listen now. Can you hear them?"

He gently touched his bow to the strings of his violin and at first I heard nothing, then, faintly as if from a great distance, I heard the chirping of a bird, then another, a little louder. I realized the bird calls were coming from the violin. Then a soft minor card sounded from the piano, then a melody.

The violin picked up the melody, and the concert had begun.

The applause erupted again, fading into silence as the music grew louder. The music continued, interrupted only by brief announcements of titles and composers, each composition more inspiring than the last, building, building to a final crescendo.

"And now, my friends," he said, "the last number on the program. There will be no encores. They could only be an anticlimax. Nor will I tell you the name of the composer, for it is unknown. And the title of the composition? That too has been worn away by the relentless winds of time. It is said that there was a time before the birth of God wherein in all the universe there was emptiness and silence, only century on century of waiting. Then, when the silence was at last ripe, a tune began to play, and the infant God awoke from His eternal sleep and began to dance, and you and I, my friends, we are the latest part of that dance, and this is that tune."

He signaled his accompanist, who fled from the stage, dropping sheet music in her haste.

Then he took his violin from under his chin, seated himself on the piano bench, thrust the violin against his groin, and began to play, stamping his foot in time to the music.

Never before had I heard such a tune, and I hope never to hear its like again. Never before had I heard such a rhythm, like the footsteps of a giant. Never before had I heard such shimmering cascades of tone showering down upon us like deadly hailstones.

Someone stood up, swaying, and began to dance in the aisle.

Then a couple, then another solo dancer.

Faith leaped to her feet, tried to drag me with her, then, when I wouldn't budge, she spun around, her hands high above her head, and was absorbed by the crowd. I think I was the last one to rise and surrender to the madness of the multitude: leaping, shaking, running like a bull in a stampede.

When I came to my senses I was out in the street and the sky was beginning to glow with the coming day. Around me I saw my townspeople, some shuffling aimlessly, some leaning against walls, a few stretched out on the ground. I knelt by one of them and felt for a pulse, but there was none. I recognized the sheriff staggering toward me. "I'll try and find the doctor," he said to me.

I left him there and headed for the parsonage.

The front door of my house stood wide open, gently swinging in the morning breeze.

I ran inside.

I stood at the foot of the hall staircase and called, "Faith! Faith! Where are you?"

There was no answer.

I wandered around the ground floor, calling for her, searching for her.

Returning to the foot of the stairs, I heard a familiar laugh. She was alive!

"Thank God," I whispered, and bounded up the steps, three at a time.

I burst into the bedroom, and there they were.

Faith and Asmodeus.

They lay naked side by side in my bed, the first light of morning gleaming on their bare, sweating skin. Faith sat up and smiled at me.

Asmodeus sat up, too, and beckoned to me, laughing. "Come join us, Parson Paul!" he called out.

"Yes," called Faith. "Come join us!"

My hand darted inside my overcoat, snatched my Colt 45 from its holster. I shot her first, right between the eyes, then him. They looked surprised. Why in God's name were they surprised?

I went to first one, then the other, feeling for a pulse. They were both dead.

I laid my gun on the dresser and sat down on the floor, back to the wall, to wait for someone to come and find us.

So here I am, a man of God, locked in a cell in the Crossroads jail. I'm charged with murder and I might as well plead guilty. If I have any consolation, it is that the demon Asmodeus will never again work his hellish spells on any innocent, unsuspecting audience. As I stand and look out through the bars in my window at the setting sun, I get to thinking about what that damn fiddle player said. Really, what was there before God was born? There must have been something. What if it really was a song? What if it was that particular song?

The setting sun flattens out into an oval, then a sliver on the horizon, then a fading glow, and there are no crickets in the desert to sing the sun to sleep.

But wait, I hear something.

By all that's holy, it's a violin playing!

And what's that click?

Oh sweet Jesus, every cell door in this jail just unlocked itself and creaked open! The music is getting louder. It's coming from the dance hall.

The other prisoners are pushing open their cell doors, shuffling out into the corridor. Me too! I'm going with them. No, no, why doesn't somebody stop us?

I'm in the street, moving in time to the music.

And there are my fellow citizens, staggering along, headed for the dance hall.

There's a dance tonight, and we'll all dance our lives away! 🦂

DUB

by Gregory Frost

illustrated by Keith Minnion

Camped that night on a wide Commanchian sandstone vista where not a speck of scrub grew nor could find purchase, as if the very land itself refuted life, Dub watched the moon come up over one protuberant crag like some monster eyeball of hellish milky cast, blind to all reason and, for that matter, reality. He'd taken off his five-gallon hat — his was a cramped cranium on the best of days — which meant that at the sight of that magnified globe he trembled in his boots with the terror of one who has the intellect of a porterhouse steak.

From where it lay upon the rough ground, the hat spoke. The sound it made was insectlike, a buzzing drone of impossible consonants and few vowels: "Bh'jrh n'lrklmmmmmnh hubba-hubba," a language spoken by no human since Noachian time, and probably not before that time either. The buzz finally penetrated Dub's imbecilic and violent dread, and he leaned over and picked up the hat and put it back on. The buzz collected into a voice — into the sneering, oracular voice that had guided Dub now for lo these past six months — guided him from out of obscurity and stupendous stupidity and into a more eminent and responsive interface with the delusory West as it was evolving. The hat spoke with particular vision, with a knowledge that he would never possess, at least not so long as he kept taking the danged thing off.

"Time to put out yer fire," said the hat, "and move on down the rills and runnels to the Valley of R'hudy."

"Is that where I'm a-goin'?"

The hat sighed in frustration. "Bruce Dern it, stop takin' me off, Dub. Every time you take me off, you git plain dumb again and have to be taught everything from the start like it's your first day with the new school marm and you've done showed up without your pants on."

Dub squinted as he tried to sift through the vituperation, finally checking to see if in fact he was wearing pants. "Okay," he said, bovine in his uncertainty.

"Good. Saddle yer Tuscaloosa and let's move on. Should reach Las Rhages afore afternoon."

He micturated upon the fire, which doused the flames. Then he gathered up his blanket and cinched the saddle to the horse, strapped on his shooting iron, and swung up behind the tooled pommel as from years of practice, thoughtlessly, as he did most everything. He rode off then into the stygian shadows in search of his destiny, which only the hat knew.

The hat had endured since the day after the dawn of time or thereabouts, though its form had altered to suit the fashion of the moment. Its first recorded appearance was among the Ookabolaponga of Madagascar, where it had taken the shape of a large spotted breadfruit and for centuries became the glabrous ritual headgear of the chief, imparting wisdom along with visions of far-off crepuscular landscapes where leviathan creatures shambled among the jagged outcrops. Its significance in the social evolution of these now-extinct people cannot be underestimated, and has been studied exhaustively by

by Gregory Frost

Professor Oliver O. Oxenfree at Arkham College, where reside as well original drawings in bat guano on stone of the Ookabolaponga chief's headdress. At some distant Ogygian moment, the cryptic chapeau was stolen by a warring tribe, and it is this event that Professor Oxenfree has linked to the demise of that small insular culture. Over centuries the hat made its way across the map of Africa where, one by one, civilizations rose and fell under its tutelage. Oxenfree's intensive studies reveal that in each case these civilizations were working toward a momentous occasion, an event unequaled in gravity and magnitude — which was to rip open some kind of temporal doorway into another realm, a chthonian dimension only hinted at in the darkest tomes, where dwell what each in their own language called "The Old Ones." Only the vagaries of existence and humankind's penchant for jealousy and appropriation of others' property had kept the rituals from completion and the race, nay, the world itself from utter destruction should these fearsome behemoths be provided ingress. The hopes of these celestial horrors depended entirely upon the successful transmission of the necessary rituals to whoever wore the hat. The hat had compatriots hereabouts, although it had failed thus far to convene with any of them.

They were, it seemed, being systematically killed off.

Most recently the hat had teamed up with an individual named Masterson, whose skill as a tough had as a result become legendary. Here the hat thought it had found someone at last who lacked any moral compass, who could be turned easily into an agent of the Elder Gods' release. And this might have been the case had the aforementioned Masterson not been dumped, cataleptically drunk, in the same alley where the fatuitous Dub had taken up residence in the shipping crate of the town's new safe. Dub saw no reason not to commandeer the lovely bowler hat that lay buzzing beside Masterson's cranium. In one swift movement, he swung apelike out of his box and snatched the thing. It sensed him — sensed him with a cosmic dread the like of which it had never known, not even in the aeons it had floated through the vast emptiness of space, seeking intelligences that it might dispose to release its infernal lords. It had once been placed briefly upon the brow of a camel, and even that diminished encephalon had proffered more possibility than the mind of Dub. Nevertheless, rules were rules, and so the hat transformed to accommodate the new cranium, and laid its plans. Dub must travel to the town of Las Rhages in the Valley of R'hudy, where the doorway to the Old Ones' world would next open. There they must be when the time was nigh, to meet whatever other worshipers were drawn by the call. To succeed, they must first stop that fiendish, shadowy bandit whose every exploit indicated that he knew of the approaching day and that he stood opposed to it; it was he who was systematically eliminating those whom the hat hoped to join. Dub must remove him — the last obstacle to the hat's wide-ranging plans. Then and only then might the new masters of this world devour these base and pathetic creatures, none of which was more base or pathetic than Dub himself.

He knew he was getting close to the town when the signs showed up. They were distanced so that he could only see one at a time along the trail. Each bore a portentous piece of a riddle, and he puzzled and worried each line until the next appeared.

When Stygian Dark has settled in,
And Uzuldaroum slimes your skin,

•

Only one thing left to do
Lift your razor from the Mnarian goo.

•

Clean it in an autoclave
Then you're ready —
•
Burma Shave.

"What's it all mean?" Dub exclaimed in a voice approaching hysteria. The hat only groaned truculently and wished for the thousandth time that it had arms that it might strangle its host.

Las Rhages proved to be the sort of one-horse town on which most of the West was formulated. That they even had one horse was impressive. That they had only one street, less so.

Dub rode in at midday, while almost everyone else lurked in umbras cast by the monolithic dwellings, some as high as two stories. He tied up his animal and sauntered up onto the walk. The walk was quite muddy, which seemed odd given the dusty dryness of the street. Antediluvian muck pulled at his boots and each lifted foot produced a sucking sound as of some tentacular behemoth disengaging itself.

DUB

One octogenarian coot sat alongside the saloon in a chair tipped back on its hind legs like a malformed creature reared up to strike, and crookedly watched Dub's approach with a grizzled eye beneath even more grizzled brows. The hat buzzed, and Dub nodded. He sucked on up to the coot. "Say, there, old timer. You tell me where I kin find the sheriff's office?"

The coot righted himself, planting his own feet squarely in the muck. "That'd be on the Mexee-kan side of town." He nodded toward the street.

Dub said, "What d'ya mean, the Mexican side? You only got one *street.*"

"Yep, one street, an' the sheriff's on the Mexee-kan side of 'er."

"That'd be t'other side, then."

The coot barked out a strange laugh, like a sea lion stuck with a fork. "You got that straight, razor, I mean, right, stranger."

Dub tipped his hat. The crown lifted. The hat warned, "Dub!"

Dub squashed the hat firmly back on his head. He turned and, grabbing the tops of his boots, pulled himself foot by foot back onto the main street, where he left a trail like that of a shoggoth oozing out of a Precambrian sea.

The sheriff's office proved easy to find. A huge radial sign hung above it, in the center of which were carved the words **OFFICE OF SHERIFF SIERRA**.

A small, leathery man swayed outside the office, attempting to sweep down the glutinous sidewalk. The tip of his broom had been snared by the ooze, and now he worked desperately to get it out. As Dub looked on, he pulled the broom free, minus half its bristles — but slipped from the effort and then plunged under the thick mud for a moment before tearing himself free of it and, clutching a post, dragged himself back to his feet. He stared unhappily at Dub from under the dripping offal. "Like a human hot fudge sundae," Dub remarked. "Only stinkier."

The hat commanded, "Go get a board, Dub," and Dub scrounged through the nearest alley until he found a piece of planking which he laid between the street and sill of the sheriff's door, then traversed the ooze by walking daintily upon it. The mud-drenched sweeper gaped at him.

Inside the office, the sheriff eyed him balefully. Sierra's ancestry seemed more amphibian than human. His huge eyes protruded from his strangely narrow head like brined eggs gone bad. The star pinned to his chest was neither brass nor bronze, but a greenish soapstone dotted with small holes.

"Kin I help you, stranger?" croaked the sheriff.

"Aw, yessir. I'm a come for the reward money — for the capture of the bandit what's been plaguing — these parts lo these many months," Dub recited as the hat dictated to him.

"You're gonna capture El Zoroaster?"

"You betcha."

Sheriff Sierra slapped the desk and laughed like a foghorn being tickled. "Son, that's the funniest thing I ever heard. You know that we've had us more bounty hunters through here to get him than you got pickles in a jar. We had us Gillman, and Rooster, and that Manco fella in just the last month."

Dub stared back like a deer caught stealing from a poor box. He swallowed. "They're here already, those fellers?"

"Sure are."

"Kin I — kin I talk to 'em?"

The sheriff scratched his wattles. "That'd depend," he said.

"Upon what?"

"Upon whether you can communicate with the dead."

When Dub only stared uncomprehendingly, he shouted, "Great Randolph Scott, son, they's all dead. Pay attention, boy. Boot Hill. Toes to the *skies!*" He began to cough in an uncontrollable fit, and blindly opened the drawer of his desk, pulled out a tin, opened it and stuck a lozenge in his mouth. After a moment the seizure passed. He looked weakly at Dub, then offered him the tin. Dub read on the lid: **Randolph Carter's Leprous Liver Pills**.

"Good fer near everything," the sheriff noted. "Don't be put off by the name." Dub took one, stuck it in his mouth, and immediately regretted it. The lozenge tasted like charred manure.

"Now, where was I," muttered Sierra. "Oh, right, all them bounty hunters is dead. And every single one had the Mark of Zoroaster branded on his patootie, and don't you think he didn't — big ol' fire-shaped burn with a 'Z' slicin' right through the middle, yessir. That's

one *mean* bandito. But, hey, you still feel like you wanna go after him, don't let me stop you now. Make my life so much easier if you succeed, and in the meantime I'll have the carpenter make another pine box. You'd be about, what, five feet six?"

"That ain't funny. I come here to open dimens—"

"Shut yer pie hole, Dub!" yelled the hat.

Dub scowled. "I'll show you. Yes I will. I'll show ya *both*. Big Z or no big Z, bring 'em on!" He stuck out his lower lip, then started away but stopped. Sheepishly, he turned back. "Sheriff, kin you tell me whar I might find a place to stay, meantime?"

The sheriff got to his feet and shambled across the room. His bulbous torso forced Dub outside as he eased himself into the doorway.

"You see across the street there, the Pnakotic Saloon?"

"Yep."

On the wall a sign read: **ROOMS $5 PER DAY**.

"Upstairs they got rooms to let."

"Anyplace a little less expensive?"

"Nope. This a one-horse town. Slim Pickens here."

"Really?"

"No, not really, but he passed through one time." Then he noticed the board on which Dub was standing. "Say, you dream that thing up?"

Dub glanced down. "Why, yes. That was me."

"That's damn clever. Maybe you ain't just a monkey-faced idiot."

"No," muttered the hat. "That's all he is."

Dub started down the board.

A passerby on the street paused to marvel at this, then saw the sheriff filling the doorway and called out, "Hi, Sierra!"

The sheriff nodded to him before wrenching himself free of the framework.

Dub took one step onto the street

when the hat said, "Bring the board with you, moron."

For a minute Dub thought about this. Then he saw the hat's wisdom and snatched the plank away from the sheriff's door.

At the Pnakotic, he shoved it across the ooze again and walked up the incline. The old coot acknowledged him by coughing up a great gob of ichor and hacking it into the muck. Then he grinned.

Dub passed through the swinging doors.

Inside, they were doing a brisk business. Men lined the bar, one foot on the rail; a poker game was going on in one corner; and an out-of-tune piano plunked away loudly enough to set his teeth on edge.

Clustered around one table sat twelve drovers, sharing a huge meal of steaks and beans. They champed and gulped like men who hadn't seen food for months and might not see it again for awhile after this. They didn't even look up as he passed by.

DON DIEGO

A dark-haired girl glided up beside him and put her arm on his shoulder. "Señor," she whispered, "you buy Tekeli-li a Corona?"

"Why, sure, I guess I'd like that."

"Dub," the hat warned, "do not get sidetracked here."

"What harm can it do?" Dub replied. "Just a little cerveza with a señorita."

"Who are you talking to?" Tekeli-li asked.

"Ahh, just talkin' into my hat, you could say." He grinned vacuously.

"Once we open the gates," the hat reminded him, "you can have her for your own slave and a hundred more just like her. This can wait."

"I'll just get you that beer, you hang on there," he told her, ignoring the hat's advice, denying it control. At the bar he asked for two beers. The bartender set down two bottles of Corona Mundi, and Dub paid him, then took the beers to her. She had picked a table away from the drovers and their collateral smell. He set down the bottles and asked, "What is it with those guys? They're on their second meal just in the time I've been in here."

"Ah, they are running a herd north to the Brucelosa spread," she explained. "They say their cook's food is an abomination to all save the creatures of Yaddith, and they call his food wagon the 'upchuck' wagon. They are leaving again tomorrow and that's what they have to look forward to for many more weeks to come, so they are eating while they can. But you, now, you're not a drover."

"No, ma'am. Never done a day's work — that is, I never drove a herd ever."

"Why, then, are you in this town?"

Dub lifted his bottle. "I'm here to kill a bandito who's named El Zoroaster," he announced, then tipped the bottle to his lips.

The saloon came to a dead stop.

Everyone in the place froze in position, with glasses half-raised to mouths, forks dripping food, tossed poker chips hovering halfway to the felt. All eyes fixed on Dub. Tekeli-li's mouth hung open, and even when a fly zipped into it, she didn't close it.

The hat sighed. "Nice goin', Marshall Dillon," it said.

Dub drank deeply from his beer, then asked, "Was it somethin' I said?"

"Naw," snarled the hat, "it's 'cause Tsathoggua and his formless star spawn just manifested on the stairs."

"Really?" Dub glanced around.

"No, not really, you mutant toad. So much for the art of surprise. We don't need to worry that Zoroaster won't know where to look for us now."

"That's a good thing, right?"

"Oh, yeah. Hell of a good thing. He's only buried three *real* gunfighters already. Sweet Pancho and Cisco, what did I do to deserve you?"

While the hat fulminated, Dub returned to his companion. "Say, I was wondering, you know, I'm lookin' for a place to stay, and well, this is kind of an expensive town, seems to me, and maybe you know somewhere cheaper than this here bar."

Tekeli-li finally closed her mouth. Then she abruptly coughed and spat out the fly. "A place to stay?"

"Yeah. Room to let, fifty cents?"

She nodded slowly, with sinister solemnity. "I know someone who could help you with *both* your causes. You need to go to the hacienda of a friend of mine."

"Nearby, is it?"

"Oh, yes, just the other side of town."

"That'd be the Mexican side?"

"Oh, you've been there?"

"Maybe."

"You go down the road to the first hacienda you come to on the right. The owner is a great man. He can put you up for a few days even."

"That's perfect," said Dub, and he silently mocked the hat for belittling him when here he was, striking out so ably on his own. "What's the gentleman's name?"

"Ah. He is our Alcalde, Don Diego de Alhazred."

"Bingo!" said the hat.

"Damme," said Dub.

"Undoubtedly," agreed the lady.

The hacienda sprawled upon the arid landscape like a shuttered mesa. It had been built upon the grounds of an old monastery, the remains of which squatted ominously down the hill from the house, its windows like roughly gouged eyes, its broken doorway a black maw of abject horror. The hat expessed a

thrill in seeing it. "I'm close now," it told Dub. "All doors shall open. All winds shall blow." Then it babbled in some ancient and guttural language, the sound mashing what little consciousness Dub possessed into pea-sized awareness. Thus the first thing he did when ushered into the hacienda was to remove the migraine-inducing, chanting Stetson fast, before it could realize his intent and stop him.

His head cleared immediately. Left on his own in the foyer, he wandered about and examined his surroundings. The hat had brought him here for some nefarious purpose, but the interior of the hacienda only invited questions, not answers. Beside the front door hung a sombrero and a pair of chaparajos, looking like the dried skin of some ichthyosaur. On another wall, beside a bookcase of ancient tomes and scrolls and dung, hung a strange plaque. Figures of froggy-fishy creatures had been worked around the edges of it. The narrow, bug-eyed faces reminded him of something familiar just out of reach of his diminutive intellect. Across the center of the plaque were carved the letters **DOODEY**.

"Boy, howdy, I wish I understood what I'm doin' here."

"What you're doing," said a voice, "is permeating my library with the stench of cow putrefaction."

Dub turned about.

The figure stood in the shadows near the doorway to the library. He wore a quilted burgundy dressing gown as if the hellish desert clime didn't bother him at all. He had a dark face, surrounded by darker hair and a short beard. He was smoking a cigar, and puffed furiously as if to drive out the cloacal stink of Dub by filling the chamber with Jamaican leaf.

"Might I ask why you've chosen to burden me with your presence?"

Dub remembered what the hat had told him to say. "Tekeli-li in town said you'd have space to rent to a poor sodbuster like mahself who's just passin' through on his way to Baja."

"She did?" He sounded truly surprised. "That speaks well for you, despite your olfactory offense. This way." Don Diego stepped back through the doorway, and so revealed that someone else had been standing behind him. It was a woman.

She had fiery red hair and strong features; in her youth she would have been diabolically beautiful, and though time had etched her face, the sight of her still robbed Dub of breath.

"Ah," said the alcalde. "This is my wife, Señora Alhazred. My dear, may I present to you . . . a friend of Tekeli-li's."

At the sound of that name, her lips compressed and she gave her husband a biting look.

"What is your name, stranger?" asked the alcalde.

"Jist plain Dub."

The señora asked, "You are here to work with my husband?" She waved at the cigar smoke, which all but entombed her.

TEKELI-LI

Dub opened his mouth to say that he was here to kill Zoroaster, but then remembered that the hat didn't want him to mention that again. He replied instead, "Oh, no, ma'am, I'm passin' through, just passin' through. Be gone tomorrow."

"Then you are a most welcome guest."

"Why, thank you, that's right decent of ya."

She smiled with effort, and moved aside as he neared.

Don Diego led him up the stairs to a second-floor wing of the house that looked as if it had been designed as a hotel. The room, containing nothing but a bed, a chair, and a wash basin, only reinforced this impression. "I shall have a pitcher of water brought to you," said Don Diego, "and some soap."

Dub now got a good look at him. His face was long and thin, aristocratic. He should have been sweating but seemed preternaturally cool and calm.

He started to close the door, but Dub thought of a clever question.

"Tell me, Señor, you ever heared of a feller name of Zoroaster?"

Don Diego's eyes narrowed, his gaze flashed. He took his cigar out of his mouth. "What an odd question. Of course I have. An ancient philosopher and magician. Why? Are you a follower of that particular cabal?"

Lost already, Dub answered, "I — I was just curious."

"Then you're likely to go the way of the cat, aren't you?" He smiled humorlessly and tried again to close the door.

"Ah, Mr. Alcaldie!" Dub said quickly. "I got one more question."

"Hello, kitty," Don Diego replied. "What else?"

"What's 'DOODEY'?"

"It is what, unless I am much mistaken, you've been rolling in for days."

"Naw," said Dub. "Well, yeah, but I mean, that plaque on your wall downstairs."

"Ah, that." He puffed for a moment, as if debating whether to tell. Dub's cretinous countenance persuaded him that there could be no harm in it. "If you must know, it stands for 'Dagon's Order of Divine Eternal Yuggoth.' Satisfied?"

"Um, not really."

"Pity." And he closed the door.

Never much given to ratiocination, Dub found the thinking necessary to winnow sense from all he'd learned too exhausting, and soon after the water and soap were delivered, he fell asleep. When he awoke it was dark in the room. The hat, lying now on the floor, was buzzing like a horde of hornets. Dub picked it up by the brim and leaned toward it as if trying to hear the ocean.

"— of all the moronic, beef-witted, fool—"

Dub pulled away. Now didn't seem a good time to put the hat back on.

He decided instead to see what his host was doing. He was hungry, and maybe they'd rustled up some decent food. He suddenly recalled the drovers in the bar and their "upchuck" wagon. He started to laugh. That was a good joke, he thought. The hat had kept him from getting it when Tekeli-li had told it to him. The hat didn't much cotton to humor: the only thing it ever laughed at was him.

He grabbed the doorknob. The door wouldn't open. He pushed at it, pulled at it, to no avail. Finally, he bent over and tried to peer through the keyhole, but there was nothing to see beyond more darkness. "Dern if they haven't locked me in."

There was nothing for it — this was more than he could solve on his own. He had to don the hat again. He dusted it lightly, smoothed the brim in the hope that this might placate it a little, then finally, reluctantly, placed it upon his head.

Immediately, it snarled, "About damn time, you idiot! What have you been doing?"

"I rested some."

"Mi-Go's gonads, we're nearing the opening of the void where all shall blend together — Ogthrod! Ogthrod! — and you take a nap."

"And we're locked in here."

The hat fell silent at this new information. Then it chuckled. "Of course we are — it's just what I thought. Don Diego *has* to be El Zoroaster. He knows we've come to kill him, thanks to your shootin' your mouth off in town. He's gonna put a stop to everything. We have to get out of here!"

"But the door —"

"To Hadoth with the door! We're goin' out by the window!"

Beneath the window, the clay tiles of the roof provided no more than a few feet of purchase, beyond which the yard below remained a black unknown. Dub wanted to protest, but the hat exercised control over him now, forcing his body up and out the window. His boots slipped on the tiles, and he clung to the window sill as he let his legs dangle over the edge.

"What if there's something under me?"

"It'll break your fall," the hat assured him.

"Break my neck, you mean."

"Shut up and let go. Would I get you killed at a time like this?"

Actually, Dub thought it probably would, but the hat made him open his fingers and he slid down the tiles and into the darkness. He hunched up in the air, and managed to land on his heels, briefly, before falling backward onto a brick surface — a circular patio with a small fountain in the center.

No one seemed to have noticed his escape. The hat had him circle the house. One window was lit, and Dub cautiously peered in to find the señora in her room, wearing nothing but a chemise. She looked as furious as an inflamed goddess. He wanted to stay but the hat forced him to move on.

Then, coming around the front of the house, he saw that lamplight emanated from the ruins of the old monastery, the source in motion inside. The hair stood up on the back of Dub's neck. The hat chuckled, "We've got him. Come on."

Dub and the hat crept down the hill. He drew his six-shooter as he approached the wide monastery doors. One of them hung by its bottom hinge only, presenting a view as if through a giant scissors. The lantern light splashed off crumbling walls and heaps of stones, off broken timbers, off sprays of hay that suggested the place had been used as a makeshift stable. High above, the roof looked to be as much patches of holes as it was tiles.

In the center of the chamber stood an

old artesian well. The large wooden lid, bigger around than a wagon wheel, had been dragged off and now leaned against a makeshift set of steps up the side of the well. The carcass of a heifer hung above the opening by a chain. It looked to have been bled. Don Diego was not in sight, but his voice echoed from somewhere deeper in the gloom: "Ry'eth tilda, kekibah! Oot-greet, Yog-Sothoth. Smeg-ma, Yog-Sothoth!" In the well, something splashed and thundered.

Dub swung one leg over the broken door. "My gawd, he's already at it, thar, hat. We gotta drill him now!"

The hat said, "Dub, wait a sec—" but it was too late to stop what it had set in motion. Dub called out, "Hey, you, Alcaseltzer or whatever, you stop that right now!"

He fired a warning shot that ricocheted off the well, then marched purposefully straight at it. "I'm puttin' you under arrest, or somethin'!"

The hat hissed, "Watch out!" and Dub narrowly avoided stepping in a massive cowpie, left no doubt by the sacrificed heifer as it realized its fatal circumstance.

The hooded face of Don Diego peeked around the well. "What are you doing here? This is *none* of your affair, cowboy, get out."

"Dub!" screeched the hat.

Dub winced at the sound. Waving his hands, he yelled, "What is it?"

Don Diego of course assumed the question was directed at him. "What is it, you ask? I'll tell you what it is." He climbed up the first step. "It is the spawn of Dagon, come to life once more, the first of the children to be reborn in our world, the return of the Eldritch Ones that your puny human brain cannot grasp!"

"He's one of *us,*" the hat hissed.

"No, he's a 'DOODEY!' " replied Dub.

Then something moved in the shadows, swinging down from the rafters like an enormous bat. It swooped at Don Diego, who, sensing the movement, turned at the last moment and received a blow to the chin that spun him about and flung him against the lip of the well. He would have spilled over the edge but the thing that had kicked him dropped onto the top step beside him and caught him by his belt.

Then it turned and grinned at Dub.

"Ha ha," came the taunting shout.

In a rare moment of lucidity, Dub cried "It's El Zoroaster!"

The caped figure, all dressed in black, with a black mask over the top half of its face, gestured rudely, snapping its arm in Dub's direction. Quite suddenly it held a branding iron that seemed to have manifested from out of the air.

"Goddam magic trick," complained the hat. "It was up his sleeve the whole time. All right, now, Dub, plug him."

"By the power of Ahura-Mazda, burn my celestial fire!" the masked man yelled. The tip of the iron ignited in a glare so bright that Dub was blinded. Closing his eyes, he saw the afterimage of the brand — the shape of a bowl filled with flames and across it all a single impressive letter **Z**.

Dub raised his arm to shield his eyes enough to squint.

El Zoroaster already had the alcalde's trousers down and with lightning speed applied the brand. Even unconscious, Don Diego de Alhazred bucked in pain as the mark scorched his buttock. Then a strange thing happened to him. His body shook, quivered like primal white jelly, and became greenishly translucent, thick, dribbling goop.

"Sakajawea, it devolved him into a

shoggoth," the hat whined. It was the first time Dub had heard fear in its voice. "Shoot him, for the love of Zoog!"

Yet even as Dub tried to take aim, the bandit shouted out, "Spenta-Mainyu!" and the branding iron ignited again. Still holding the rope, he swung from the steps. Dub's shot went wide and plooched into the gelatinous corpse of the alcalde. He stumbled back, stepped in the cowpat he'd missed earlier and skidded sideways onto his hip. The masked bandit landed just behind him. Dub jumped up and tried to run, but even as he took his first step he saw the brand being driven home. His reaction was instinctive, pure self-preservation. Just as the brand reached him, he grabbed his hat and covered his butt. There was a purple flash and a shriek, and El Zoroaster flew back all the way to the well. He struck it with a loud smack. The side of the well cracked. Ever so slowly, like a great indecisive hunk of yeti on a cliff, it toppled. First one chunk, then another, the whole rim collapsing in, crushing and burying whatever ancient horror the alcalde had drawn forth.

Dub meanwhile discovered that the crown of his hat had burned straight through.

The shriek — a sound made by no human organ of speech — went on and on as the hat tore itself from Dub's grasp. On the floor it lost its Stetson shape and flowed into a truer form, a tentacled flopping batrachian thing that was mostly mouth and teeth. And eyes. Fiendish, cyclamen eyes. The mouth, twisted in a sneer, snarled, "You loathsome, spotty imbecile, I'm melting, oh, my beautiful wickedness, my Old Ones, my sphincter! All destroyed by you! Oh, the *humanity!*"

It shriveled as it raged until no more than a patch of leathery tendril remained and that, finally, ceased to move.

El Zoroaster groaned and tried to stand. He had lost his mask, and Dub recognized him. "Why, you're that little street sweeper from town!"

The bandit tried to gesture nonchalantly but in doing so he collapsed face down again. Dub holstered his pistol and helped the bandit up.

"That's some clever disguise yah got."

"Thank you, and you are the clever cowpoke with the board," El Zoroaster wheezed. "I think my ribs are broken."

"Shuckidarns, you'll be fine. I'll git you up to the hacienda there and we'll take care of you."

"But the Señora — I mean I just killed her husband."

Dub pursed his lips while he thought. "Well," he said after awhile, "we just won't mention that part."

"Would you — would you consider being my disciple? I have little luck finding disciples."

"Disciple. Is that like a dreamsicle?"

The bandit blinked and seemed to focus upon Dub's beady countenance for the first time. He said, "Never mind."

"Okey," Dub replied, infinitely happy not to have to think.

In the end, Señora Alhazred was all too willing to patch up the bandit. She had despised her husband's necromantic doings and was delighted that he had vanished in so convenient a fashion. "He was a slug long before you got to him," she told El Zoroaster as she tenderly wrapped his ribs.

Dub left the bandit and the lady breakfasting on the patio. He took the sombrero from the wall, but ensured that it did not speak before donning it, then saddled his Tuscaloosa and rode off into the sunrise. He thought he might go back east, back to his hometown of Squamous, Mass. He hadn't been there since childhood. He thought he might look up his old friend, Joe Curwen, a level-headed cayuse if ever there was one. The Wild West, thought Dub, was just too full of things eldritch and unnameable for him — especially the unnameable part.

THE THREE GRAY WOLVES

by JIM HARMON

illustrated by P. Domain

That story of yours was a humdinger, Partner. They found the doggie on top of the barn. Yes sir, a humdinger. That calls for another round. Hey, barkeep! Me? Well, I got no story as good as yours, but — Well, I could tell you about the three gray wolves.

It all started one twilight about five or six months ago. I was on my bed in the bunkhouse, listening to Shorty's radio. He says this is 1933 and we got a right to all the modern inventions. So he's got this battery Philco all hooked up, some wires struck between the bunkhouse and the cook shack. He was pulling in this station from Detroit. "All the way to Oklahoma from Detroit, Jake."

I marveled at it, the way he wants. But I can't say I think much of the show he likes so much.

This show is about a cowpoke who wears a mask and just goes around looking for trouble. If he's wearing a mask, anybody he meets is going to pump lead into him, front, back or sideways, and I don't think his career would be too long. For a pard, he's got this Injun. Lots of Injuns would make good pards, and I've ridden with a few of them myself for a time. But he keeps sending this Injun into barrooms to hang around and see if he can find some trouble for this masked fellow to get mixed into. Well, if he is like a lot of Injuns I know, he sure would enjoy that job, but I don't know how much information he would be bringing back.

Well, I'm getting tired of listening to Shorty's favorite show, so I tells him I think I'll go out for a little ride, maybe check some fences. Shorty is too busy

listening to pay me much mind.

I saddle up ol' Skunk and get ready for a little ride. I guess I had been in the saddle about twelve hours that day, but I traded off from Skunk about noon, and he was well rested.

With night coming on, I knew the one spot no Lazy J cowboy would go was over towards the Hanging Tree. But I thought of this masked waddie on the radio who just went looking for trouble. I could be like him. Playing it safe had never put a dollar in my pocket so far.

Now you understand I didn't really believe in haunts. I think a lot of other cowboys didn't really believe in them either. They sort of pretended they did, probably to put a scare into some of the newer hands, watch them jump at a coyote howl or whatever. But there is that feeling down deep — maybe there was something to the business about the haunts.

It sort of put a little edge to my ride. Not that I really believed it.

So Skunk and I started over towards the Hanging Tree on the north road. It was bright moonlight and cool as night drew on, and it was a mighty nice ride.

Sure enough, before long there was the Hanging Tree with black limbs reaching up towards the stars like a pair of hands stretching up, begging for something. Maybe for mercy on the black souls sent to their maker from that tree.

They were still there on the lower limb — the three ropes tied to the limb, with lengths of cut strands hanging down. It had been so many years since the three gray wolves had been hanged — no, not critters, but three men who was called Wolves, and real bad ones too. It was sort of an insult to the honest four-legged wolves who only killed what they needed to live. These two-legged varmints could never get enough of killing and taking everything they could rustle. Until that night when the posse caught up with them. Must have been forty years ago, so it didn't seem likely that those ropes would not have rotted away. Some of the boys said somebody must have replaced those ropes in more recent years, just to sort of keep the story alive. In any case, the cut ropes from the hangings were there still there, or so it seemed.

The limb hung out over the road and it did give you a funny feeling in your backbone to ride under the hanging ropes.

"It would be nice to have some company, Skunk," I observed.

"You ain't alone Cowboy," a voice said.

That voice gave me a start, hot blood rushing through me. I turned in the saddle and I saw these three gents on their horses right behind me. I hadn't heard them ride up at all, too busy with my own thoughts, I guess.

I gave the group a wave. "There's four of us then. At least nobody is going to take us for the three haunts."

A ripple of laughter went through the group. "There's sure not *four* haunts here," a second man said.

I wondered if they had been standing there in the shadow of the tree. I sure did not hear them ride up. They looked like cowboys but even in the moonlight, I could see they had pale complexions, looking almost gray by the moon. Any real cowboy would have been tanned all to hell. *Townies,* I said to myself. Townies just waiting to pull some of their slicker stuff on me, and get my money. Not hardworking cowhands like myself.

I only had three silver dollars in the pocket of my Wranglers, and two paper dollars in my sock, but they might have thought I had my month's pay and was heading for town to spend it. Not that my pay was much more than my savings.

"Well, I'll be riding on, boys," I told the riders. "I don't find this spot none too cheerful."

"Neither do we," said the leader, Black Hat. "We'll ride along with you."

"It's a free country," I said.

We rode along apiece in the bright of the night, and I noticed something else about these untrustworthy townies. Their horses were making no perceptible sound. Only Skunk's hooves were clattering on. I read in one of Pecos' magazines a story about riders who had rubber shoes on their horses, and they made no sound. I had never seen that, but I knew in snow country you could wrap a horse's hooves in leather tie-ons and it made their footing easier, and just coincidentally-like, it made the hooves silent. Just right to sneak up on folks and catch them unawares.

It was bright, but not bright enough for me to make out whether these boys had their horses' hooves wrapped.

We were leaving the Hanging Tree behind, and I was kind of feeling antsy about riding along without saying nothing, like we were attending a funeral. "I guess those old boys back there got what they deserved forty years back," I said.

Laughter rippled through the group. "I opine they did," said Black Hat.

"The way I heard it they wiped out all the men on a pack train bringing supplies to the starving town of Grover," I said.

One of the other men, Mr. Beard, chimed in. "Maybe the Wolves had to eat too. Ain't funny going for days without food in your belly."

"They might have tried working for their supper," I said. "You don't have to do murder just to get something to eat."

Mr. Beard started to say something and Black Hat waved him down.

"Those were pretty desperate times, Stranger. The Three Wolves had a bad reputation on them. I don't expect anybody would give them a job to earn their keep."

I snorted, almost as loud as Skunk does sometimes. "So they had to gun down half a dozen men who had done them no mischief? I can't forgive that."

The third of the riders spoke up — the Kid. "What do you know of forgiveness?"

"I am not highly qualified in the subject. I go to church on Christmas and Easter, and I hear about forgiveness. But I got to admit, if somebody does me wrong I want to get back at him."

Just then in the moonlight I saw a jackrabbit cross our trail, and then just stop on the other side of the road, as if looking at somebody or listening for something, as animals will do.

I reined in Skunk. "Now if I just had my Winchester with me, I could bag that pufftail, skin him, build a little fire and we fellers could have a moonlight grub session."

Black Hat pulled back his coat. "No Winchester, but here's a Colt."

Bagging a rabbit with a handgun isn't easy, but some can do it. Black Hat tried it. His six-shooter made the softest

P. Domain

sound I ever heard from the mouth of a shooting pistol.

"Must be something wrong with your powder," I said. "There he goes."

"The powder is old," Black Hat said. "I had forgot how old. It made it seem as if the bullet had no weight, no substance, wouldn't you say, my friend?"

The other two laughed a little.

"Well, it sure didn't bother Mr. Bunny none, that's all I know," I told him.

I was feeling a little better now. If their weapons were no better than that, these fellers weren't going to try to rob me. They might have some idea in mind of slickering me out of my silver.

We rode on for a while. I was getting a little uneasy with the silence.

"Too bad about the fellers who got hung, the Three Wolves," I said.

"They sure loused themselves up killing those pack train men and then getting themselves strung up for it."

"It was too bad," said Black Hat.

"Of course, the posse couldn't have known about the amnesty. News traveled slow in those days."

"Amnesty? What amnesty?" the Kid demanded.

"Well, as I understand it, back in 1872 the governor proclaimed a general amnesty on all crimes committed before Midnight April 25, that year. Even the raid on the pack train came a few hours before that. If the posse knew that, they were supposed to let 'em free if they laid down their arms and become productive citizens. Supposed to, unless their blood was heated too much by then."

The three men sat still as window store dummies in their saddles.

Finally, Black Hat spoke. "Then the Three Wolves were forgiven, have been forgiven for over forty years?"

"Ironical, ain't it?"

"Our trails part here," the leader said. "May fortune always favor the bringer of the news."

The three men rode off. Funny how silent their mounts were. I checked the three silver dollars in my pocket. They were still there. Those townies had seemed awful sharp. I wasn't sure they hadn't fished those cartwheels out somehow when I wasn't looking.

Speaking of dollars, how about we flip for this round, Friend? You call it.

Heads? Let's see. Nope, tails. I win. Funny about that. I always win. I mean, well, I almost always win.

I know it wasn't much of a story. I guess you had to be there. Sure was a spooky feeling riding past the Hanging Tree and running into those three. But it sure can't compare to your story. The calf was right on top of the barn, you say?

ALLEN K.

SPUD WRANGLER

by Kent Patterson

illustrated by Allen Koszowski

With the suddenness of a rifle shot, a desert thunderclap rumbled and rolled across the Idaho plains. Here and there scattered rain drops fell, kicking up tiny puffs of dust where they hit the dry ground.

"That there were a close 'un," drawled old Parley McKonky. Clucking gently, he reined in his horse. "Now, now, there, there," he said, patting the horse's neck. "Just a little desert storm, and it ain't agoin' to eat you." The horse trembled, its nostrils flared and its eyes went wide with fear.

Brig Clark's horse stood placidly as a cardboard cow. Couldn't even hear it thunder, Brig thought with disgust. Of course they always gave the oldest horse to the newest wrangler. A fourteen year old boy got treated nothing better than a baby when wranglers were concerned. He glanced at Parley. The old man's face was as wrinkled as a outcropping of lava. Hat off, head raised, he sniffed the air. So did his horse.

"Boy, there's trouble brewing." He looked at Brig. "You're going to earn a wrangler's pay today. That lightning hit close. Real close. Somewhere around Twin Missionaries Springs. Now tell me what you smell."

Brig sniffed. He smelled mostly horse, sage brush, and maybe a touch of grungy underwear. He took off his hat and tried again. There was something else. The musty scent of desert rain. And something else yet, a faint aroma which reminded him of his mother's kitchen.

"That's the smell a spud wrangler fears most, son." Parley gave him a keen glance. "That smell, son, is baked potato." He raised his hand for silence. "Put your ear to the ground, boy, and listen."

Brig climbed down from his horse. Holding the reins in one hand, he lay flat. Raindrops speckled the dirt with little brown craters. Brig placed his ear on the ground and strained to hear. He heard leather reins creaking, the hoarse breathing of his horse. *A hoarse horse,* he thought wildly.

Then he heard it. Not a sound, really, but a trembling in the ground.

"That's a stampede, son, and it's coming our way." Parley lit a cigarette, the smell of tobacco permeating the air. "They're a-coming our way, and they're coming hard. And there ain't one damned thing between them and Snake River Canyon but you and me."

An image of Snake River Canyon flashed through Brig's mind. You popped over a little ridge and there it was, a sheer cliff of black lava dropping four hundred feet straight down. He'd seen a horse fall off it once. Ants had eaten the remains. There wasn't a piece big enough to interest anything else.

"That herd's the entire year's crop." Parley looked at Brig. "If the panic spreads to the main herd, which it will if we don't stop it —" his voice dropped off. "Well, it'll be a mighty long, hungry winter in Idaho. We got maybe two hours."

"But I don't have a watch."

"Take a look at where the sun is," said Parley, pointing to the sun which just now burst out from behind the storm cloud. "See where it's going to hit Hanged Man Spike?"

Brig looked. Hanged Man Spike was a lava outcropping that stabbed into the Western sky like a broken tooth.

"By the time the sun hits the Spike, the herd will hit the Canyon."

"What we going to do?" Brig asked, ashamed at the quaver in his voice.

"We got us a few minutes to spare. I'm finishing my smoke. You, well, boy, if you got to go, you better go now. You might not get a better chance all day."

Brig looked around for a rest room, or even a tall bush. Nothing for miles except tumbleweeds, scanty patches of cheat grass, and knee-high sage brush stretching off in all directions in rows as neatly as if it had been planted. He took a deep breath, unzipped, and peed standing in the open desert like a man, leaving a miniature Snake River Canyon in the dust.

He remounted his horse, pulled an Idaho Spud candy bar from his saddle bag, split the wrapper with a single thrust of his thumbnail like his daddy had taught him, and began to eat. The rich, chocolate marshmallow taste mixed with the flavor of horse and desert dust.

Now the air reeked with the smell of baked potato.

The ground trembled. Brig munched his candy bar. Control yourself, he told himself. Real wranglers don't sweat. He stole a glance at Parley, puffing his smoke calmly as if the stampede were a radio show on a station he couldn't get.

Now the trembling in the ground shook the air. Parley's horse pranced back and forth, rolling the whites of its eyes and sawing its mouth against the bit.

Even Brig's horse lifted its head and whinnied, staring off to the north where a low ridge of lava blocked the view. "Finally something woke you up," Brig whispered to the horse. "I thought you was dead."

The rumbling became a roar. Now even Parley stared at the giant clouds of dust billowing up in the North. He glanced at Brig. "You ready, son?" he shouted over the roar.

Not trusting himself to speak, Brig nodded.

"Remember, boy. We're all there is between the herd and the canyon. We don't turn 'em, you know the only thing we'll need?"

A brown tidal wave of potatoes burst over the low lava ridge. A flood of Idaho Number One Bakers the size of bread loaves, tumbling end over end, eyes white with panic.

Parley's last few words died in the thunder of the stampede. But the joke was ancient, and Brig knew it well. If the herd went over the canyon wall, all a spud wrangler needed was five hundred tank cars of gravy.

"Ki yi yee yee, roll you bakers roll!" Parley shouted the traditional cry of the spud wrangler. His horse shot forward like a cannonball. Through the last of his candy bar, Brig tried shouting too, but his mouth was so dry he only succeeded in spraying himself with chocolate marshmallow and bits of coconut. He glanced at the hordes of potatoes now streaming through every gap in the lava ridge and rolling down the plain as irresistibly as Noah's flood. His horse whinnied in fear and, in spite of Brig tightening the reins, she shied backwards, away from the thunder of the onrushing spuds. "You're making a coward of me, horse," Brig said.

But it was him making a coward of himself. He whose sweaty hands slipped on the reins, whose breath came short, whose pulse pounded like Satan's own trip hammer in his brain. He tried to yell a "Ki yi yi" but the sound turned to dust and chocolate in his mouth.

Spur your horse, spur you coward, he screamed in his mind. But try as he might, his spurs seemed to have a will of their own. Unbidden, tears sprang to his eyes. Bless the Lord that Parley was halfway across the flat and couldn't see.

Turn back. Get out of here. For a second he decided to give the horse its head, race away from that implacable, thundering mass of spuds, get away and live.

But, even as his horse turned, an image flashed through his mind: wranglers gathered around the chuck wagon after a hard day's work. Tired, aching, maybe hurt, but each knowing he'd done his share, that he'd never let a partner down. The Idaho sunset, turning the desert purple and pink, with maybe a single puff of cloud flaring gold in an empty sky. Night slipping across the desert plain, the camp fire crackling, smelling of sage. A couple of prime Idaho Number Ones turning on a spit, the comforting sound of male voices laughing, joking about big spuds and beautiful women.

If he turned away now, he would never be one of them. Oh, no one would say a thing. Not by a whisper, not by a hint, would anyone breath the word "coward." No one would have to.

But in the morning when he woke up he'd find a potato peeler by his bed. There was nothing written down, but the rule was iron. Men herded spuds. Cowards were only fit for making french fries.

Brig closed his eyes. "Ki yi yee yee," he squeaked. He opened his eyes and shouted louder. "Ki yi yee yee!" Louder yet! He spurred his horse. It shied. He spurred harder. *"Ki yi yee yee!"* he screamed at the top of his voice. "Roll on, you bakers." Hooves drummed on the dry desert dust as his horse headed for the rampaging herd of potatoes.

Minutes turned into hours, days, as Brig charged down the long lines of the potato herd. Screaming, shouting, waving his arms and brandishing his long, black spud-masher, he and Parley drove the huge, lead spuds back. If these turned, the herd followed, rumbling along like a freight train. But sometimes the lead spuds resisted even the masher; and then Brig would resort to the spud wrangler's greatest and

most ancient weapon, holding his arms overhead in the mystical half circle that for reasons unknown drove terror into the very starch of even the toughest tuber. That always worked, though no spud wrangler knew why.

Dust billowed high into the sky, the few sprinkles of rain long since dried out in the blazing summer sun. Brig pulled his bandanna over his nose and mouth. Dust covered him until he and his horse looked like some grey monster out of the past.

But the herd turned. Gradually, the spuds in the lead circled, sweeping their followers into a gigantic spud whirlpool. Hoarse with shouting, his face caked with dust, Brig felt like a hero, a genuine spud wrangler at last.

In the distance, he saw Parley riding up fast, waving his arms and yelling words lost in the thunder of the spud herds.

So what now, Brig thought. The work's nearly over. He couldn't make out what Parley was saying. "How we doing?" he shouted as Parley came up.

"Run for your life!" Parley shouted.

Only then did Brig notice the rumbling of the spud herds had taken on a deeper, throbbing, more menacing sound. He looked to the north. Over the ridge came a solid wall of bakers which blotted out the sky. Brig had never seen spuds panicked like that, climbing on top of each other to get away. He knew this could only be the main herd, the livelihood of half the state. It was a spud avalanche, a city of spuds set up on edge and stampeding across the Idaho plains. Parley streaked towards the high ground of Mormon Butte. Brig followed.

He didn't have to urge his horse to run. However old and tired, she was a spud horse and knew all too well what that ground-shaking roar meant.

Brig didn't look back. He could sense that towering mass looming over him.

A shadow slipped over his head. The potato herd blocked out the sun. Now he was on the welcome slopes of Mormon Butte. Higher! He had to get higher up the slope to be safe, "Come on, old gal," he urged on his horse. "Just a few more steps."

He glanced back as the great wave of potatoes crested high over his head. "Jump for your life!" he shouted, driving in his spurs. With one great convulsive heave, his horse leaped just as truckloads of spuds smashed down.

"Good horse, great horse!" She stood shivering, foam spuming down her flanks. High on Mormon Butte, they were safe for the moment. Brig watched the masses of spuds surging by. Thousands had been broken or mashed. The air reeked with hot starch. The horse's flanks rose and fell.

"Parley!" Brig shouted. Parley lay flat on the ground on his back. One hand held his horse's reins. Brig dismounted, leading his horse, and ran up to Parley.

Parley stared at the blank sky. One arm jutted out at an impossible angle. A trickle of blood ran from his mouth.

"Parley, you're hurt."

"Don't mind me, kid. Mind the herd."

"But there's too many of them."

Parley coughed, and stared at the sky. Then he spoke.

"They're scared, son. Just plain blind panicked. And a scared spud can't see beyond the sprouts of its eyes. It's barely an hour now till they hit Snake River Canyon. Take my horse. It's faster. You've got to stop them. Everything's up to you now." Parley turned his head.

"What do I do, Parley? How can I get them to turn?" He looked down at the ocean of spuds. Nothing could turn that herd.

"Only one way to turn a herd of scared spuds, son," Parley said. "Get there first and find something to scare them worse than the lightning did. Now git. Go."

Without a word, Brig mounted Parley's horse and spurred along Mormon Ridge. The ridge, he knew, ran south-east a couple of miles, then petered out. He had to flank the spuds, run along the ridge until he could get in front of them,then drop down to the plain. He glanced over his shoulder at the sun. Hanged Man's Spike nearly touched the round red disk.

He could get ahead of the spuds, but then what? How could a lone boy turn a herd that skunked even real wranglers? The horse's hoof-beats drummed in his head like some mocking song. You got to find something to scare them worse than the lightning did.

But what? Certainly not a lone boy on a horse. They'd trample him to pink gravy. What scared a spud? What could possible be worse for a spud than being baked in a lightning bolt? It had to be something big, something terrible.

Brig tried to remember the stories his daddy had told him, stories handed down by spud wranglers since the earliest days. Many of the legends predated the arrival of the white man, and more often than not made no sense in the modern world. Stories about how the Quetzal flew the spirit of the potato northward from South America, or how an ancient tuber tribe went mad in the canyon lands of what was now Utah. Brig had never been interested in his father's stories, but now he wished he had paid more attention. There might have been a tidbit of wisdom in there that could help him now.

He could barely hear himself think over the roar of the stampede and the hoof-beats of Parley's horse, but he noticed with grim satisfaction that he was gaining on the herd. He could beat them to the canyon, but what could he do once he got there?

There was one thing that always scared a potato: the half-circle of arms over the head. No one knew why it struck such fear into the hearts of spuds, but its effect was undeniable. It was such a primal image to a spud that any kind of half-circle would make them skittish. Something as simple as an arched gateway could keep a ranch house's yard free of even the boldest spud.

Yes, the half-circle would scare a spud, but this herd was so vast that most of the spuds would never see him making the sign. He needed something bigger, and in the failing evening light, he needed something that would shine out like a beacon to the advancing herd.

There was only one chance. Joe Handy's construction crew. Brig had seen him working at the new Big Falls market just yesterday. He'd be working today. Brig glanced back at Hanged Man's Spike. If there were only more time!

He had managed to flank the herd. Coming down on to the plain, Brig knew what he had to do. The herd would follow the plain to hit Snake River Canyon about three miles from Big Falls City. He had to get to the City first, grab Joe Handy, then get there before them. There wasn't a second to waste.

His mouth set, Brig spurred towards Big Falls City.

"Man, you're plum loco!" Under the dust, Joe's face showed white as a sheet. Actually whiter than a spud wrangler's sheets. Standing on the bed of his ancient Ford pickup, Joe tightened the connections to a portable generator. "I'm on duty, and I ain't supposed to leave my place. And this," he pointed to the contents of the truck, "is supposed to run 24 hours a day."

"Yeah, well, get it running now," Brig snapped. In the west, Hanged Man's Spike speared the bottom of the sun.

"I ain't staying here. Them spuds'll push you right over the edge of the canyon."

The air shook with the rumble of the advancing spuds. A column of dust marked the herd. In maybe five minutes they'd be here. But the herd was tiring. That was good.

"You just get that equipment working. I'll be the one throwing the switch."

Brig wiped his brow. Involuntarily, he glanced over the canyon edge. Four hundred feet straight down to a black rock floor. Far below he could see buzzards wheeling in the updraft. From here, they looked no bigger than gnats.

This had better work. If it didn't, mashed potato city, with Brig on the bottom. Bring on the gravy.

He looked back up just as the electrician's broad back disappeared over a lava outcropping to the east.

Damn! What a coward. For a second, Brig considered joining him. Then he jumped into the bed of the pickup and slapped Parley's horse on its rump. "Run for your life, boy." The horse bolted after the electrician. Brig hated to see it go, but if this didn't work and he went over the side of the canyon, the boss would resent losing a good horse.

Suddenly the spud herd burst into view. Not as tired as Brig had hoped. In front of them, frightened jackrabbits and a lone coyote scampered.

Brig pressed the Start button on the generator motor. Damn. Nothing. The wall of spuds came nearer. Now Brig could smell the starch.

Forcing himself to stay calm, Brig tested each wire on the generator. Now the thundering spuds drowned all other sounds. Running at full speed, a jackrabbit thudded into the pickup's side and dropped to lie quivering in the dust.

A wire came lose in Brig's hand. Bad connection. He glanced up, and gasped. All he could see was a wall of spuds. His sweaty fingers shoved the wire into place, and he jabbed the starter button.

The generator's engine whirred, coughed, and quit.

The reek of hot starch and potato peels clogged Brig's nostrils. The first few spuds splattered against the side of the pickup.

Brig jabbed the start button again.

The engine whirred, coughed, then roared into life. Quickly Brig flipped the light switch to "on."

From the very edge of Snake River Canyon, two gigantic golden arches lit up the Idaho sky. They were just yellow marquee lights on a wire frame, but they stood out stark and bold against the blackness beyond.

The oncoming herd recoiled. In a twisting, seething mass of brown, spuds bounded backwards, piling on top of the herds still streaming in from the plain. A mountain of spuds reared into the sky, looming over the low plain like some new volcanic cone.

Then, gradually, the mass turned on itself, the herd streaming back north, northeast, northwest — any direction to escape those terrible glittering golden arches.

Exhausted, Brig stepped down off the pickup and lay down in the warm ,starch-smelling dust. He closed his eyes, wondering if spud wranglers would ever learn why the occult and archetypal symbol struck such fear into the hearts of spuds.

"Brig. Ya OK, son?"

Brig opened his eyes. Parley stood over him, bandages covering his chest. His arm lay in a sling.

"Parley. I thought you was dead."

"Not hardly, son."

"How are the . . ."

"The spuds? Well, I reckon they're about ten miles out in the desert by now, and a tireder and more docile pack of tubers you ain't never going to see in your life." Parley grinned. "Let the tenderfeet and the little boys round 'em up." He pulled a silver flask and an Idaho Spud candy bar from his saddle bag. "We wranglers got some serious resting to do."

From the hell-hole hangars of the Himalayas hurtle:

FLAMING DEVILS OF THE AIR
An exciting book-length novel

by Antoine de Saint-Exupéry & Robert J. Hogan

Plus two thrilling novelettes:

THE DEADLY GASBAGS OF AH-CHU-FUNG
by Robert Leslie Bellem

REVENGE OF THE HYDROGEN HORDE
by Col. Sean "Bucky" Wallace

Don't miss the incredible April issue of

Spicy Oriental Zeppelin Stories

GOING AFTER YEECHIPHOOIE

by David Sherman

illustrated by David Grilla

"Spaghetti!" howled Mad Cow Brazos when he saw the red-drenched strings Cookie slopped into his tin dish. "Spaghetti fer brekfas'? *Agin?!?*"

"Sho' 'nuff beats jeller fer brekfas'," Hung Dawg Hooligan snarled from next to Brazos. "Out'n mah way, "Ah'm hungered som'pin fierce."

Hooligan sharply elbowed Mad Cow in the ribs to move him from in front of the steaming vat from the stygian depths of which Cookie ladled his spaghetti. Mad Cow shot Hung Dawg a look that if it was from his .44 would have sprayed bits and pieces of bloody bones and gore over most of the visible landscape. Instead, he snarled and moved out of the way.

"It's 'cause *som'*un fergot t' load the beans 'n bacon onta the chuck wagon," said Buzzard Bait Northrop, not to be confused with Buzzard *Breath* Northrop, to whom he was distantly related through his mother's second-cousin-twice-removed's side of the family.

Cookie's head jerked toward Buzzard Bait, the swarm that constantly buzzed about his face seeking the effluvia that dripped into his beard when he tasted his cooking reorganized and followed his head so rapidly they hardly missed a drip. Thanks to the conscientious ministrations of the flies, Cookie had the cleanest beard of any of the cow-pokers, card-barracudas, and back-shooters who made up the posse searching for Yeechiphooie, the ancient Zinni god recently reincarnated and terrorizing the good folk of West Archaic, Arizona Territory.

"T'ain't mah fawlt!" Cookie snapped at Buzzard Bait. "Heavy Thumb Trump dun gone 'n mis-labeled the barrels. Ah tol' him Ah wanted a mixed barrel o' pinto beans and great northerns. 'N tha's what the lable on the barrel says. Yah kin see it fer yersef, ya wanna look." He faced front again and slopped a ladle-full of spaghetti and sauce into Hung Dawg Hooligan's dish. "If'n ya could read," he added softly, with a side-glance at Buzzard Bait Northrop.

"Ugh, me like'um spaghetti," Red Fork Wathahiya said loudly as he sidled up to the steaming vat. "Spaghetti sauce good! Look like clotted blood. *Taste* like clotted blood. Me like'um." Scorpion Stung Shaunessey and Buffalo Apple Cranston, who stood to Wathahiya's sides in the chuck line, edged away from the Injun.

Cookie shot Red Fork a dirty look but ladled an extra large portion into is dish when he got to the head of the line, not only because Red Fork liked his cooking but because Wathahiya was the only Zinni who agreed to help the posse track down Yeechiphooie.

It began a month earlier, when Thrown Shoe Hammerforge was woken by the panicked whinnying of the horses in his livery stable. Hammerforge had jumped out of bed in his nightdress and stocking cap, stepping directly into his carpet slippers which were placed where they always were right where he could step into them if he had to suddenly rise in the middle of the night. Thus dressed, Thrown Shoe raced out of his house which was situated immediately next to the stable and saw to his wonder a six-foot-long

by David Sherman

arrow quivering in the front wall of the stable.

Before he could do anything about it, a hideous and hideously loud laugh attracted his attention. He looked to his left and *lo!* not two hundred yards away, standing in the light of the full moon, stood a ten-foot-tall Injun holding a bow! The Injun grinned at Hammerforge, showing teeth from which unspeakable oozings dripped from unutterable things caught between them and drew a threatening finger across his throat. With a thoroughly maniacal hideous and hideously loud laugh, the Injun disappeared. It was only then that Thrown Shoe realized the Injun hadn't cast a shadow in the brilliant moonlight!

A *whoosh* right next to Hammerforge caught his attention. The still-quivering arrow had burst into flames and the stable wall was catching on fire!

"Far! FAR!" Thrown shoe shouted at the top of his lungs and ran into the stable to open the stalls and lead the panicked beasts out.

In minutes a dozen townsfolk were with him, leading the last of the cayuses out of danger and rounding up the frightened nags that had come out when nobody was yet there to corral them. None of the saddle or dray animals were lost, but the stable burned to the ground, and it was all the bucket brigade could do to keep the flames from devouring Hammerforge's house along with the stable.

No sooner had the livery stable been rebuilt than the mysterious Injun came back in the middle of the night and burned down Heavy Thumb Trump's general store and the house where lived the good Parson Mather and his daughter Cassandra. The very night after the townsfolk ot those two edifices rebuilt the dastardly and, the people were now thinking, probably supernatural Injun reappeared and burned down the Fat Chance saloon, the Ante Up gambling hall, and Quick Cut's barber shop. The loss of the Fat Chance and the Ante rightly riled up the cow-pokers, card-barracudas, and back-shooters around West Archaic who relied on them for entertainment and (for the card-barracudas) income and the call rose for the sheriff to come from Archaic and do something about the situation.

Sheriff Shothip limped off the Ghoulhound Lines stage coach three days later, saw all the new construction, and announced, "Don't look t' me like you got no problems heah," and got right back on the stage coach and told the driver to turn around and take him back to Archaic. When the driver protested that he had a schedule to keep and was due in Shantak in two hours which he'd never be able to do if he turned around and went back to Archaic now, Sheriff Shothip drew his Colt Peacemaker, pointed it at the driver, and said, "Ah said, take me back t' Archaic, mah business heah is finished," the driver said, "Yassah," and turned that stage coach right around and headed back to Archaic, running down little Billy Bonnie's puppy and almost trampling old Miss Kitty in his haste to do the sheriff's bidding. (Little Billy Bonnie was so distraught at the untimely demise of his beloved puppy caused by Sheriff Shothip's haste to return to Archaic that he bore a lifelong disdain for the forces of law and order, and turned henceforth to banditry most foul.)

It was soon after that that Rybekka Ramrodder stood forth in the midst of West Archaic's main street (truth be told West Archaic's only street) and bellowed out in a voice to rattle the dead and possibly raise the recently dead, "Who heah's man enuff t' come with me and hunt that Injun down?"

For awhile there it look like no one was up to the challenge, that not another man was man enough to face the monstrous Injun who was terrorizing West Archaic. Rybekka Ramrodder began cursing and was about to turn away when Catastrophy Annie hitched up her bustle, gave the top of her bustier a yank, and stepped into the street. She walked up to Ramrodder and put a hand on his arm to stop him from leaving, then faced the crowds, withering like bushes in a drought. "If'n there's nobody *man* enough, mebbe there's some who are *wimmen* enough t' hunt thet Injun down!" she screeched.

Catastrophy Annie was not a rough-and-tumbler, and the only shooting iron she had any familiarity with was a dainty derringer she kept in a holster on her wrist, under the sleeve of her dress. But she and her girls were having a hard time of it until the Fat Chance saloon got rebuilt.

The only accommodations they'd been able to find during the reconstruction was the spare room in Parson Mather's new house. "Do you have any idea how *hard* it is to entertain customers in a *parson's* house?" she demanded of Zitz Fleiss when he demanded to know why business was off. "There is *five* of us and only *one* bed, so's we *cain't* entertain more 'n two at a time — if'n we kin sneak 'em past the parson. And when we do, that skinny dotter of his, that Cassandry, keeps poking her head in 'n shriekin' 'bout how disaster's comin'!" Catastrophy Annie didn't believe the supernatural Injun would stop bothering them once he burned down every building in West Archaic, but that he'd burn down the new buildings as well. She knew then she'd have to pack up and head for another town, and there just weren't that many empty cribs left in the Arizona Territory.

Her ploy worked, and soon enough Mad Cow Brazos, Hung Dawg Hoo-

COOKIE

ligan, Buzzard Bait Northrop, Sidewinder Calhoun, Ace Up His Sleeve Beauregard and enough other cowpokers, card-barracudas, and backshooters stepped up to form a right strong posse.

"Okay, Rebecca, how we gonna go after this Injun?" Skunk Beansworth asked when it was obvious nobody else was going to volunteer.

"Don't call me Rebecca!" Ramrodder roared. "It's *Rybekka!*" His eyes turned the red of hellfire, and the steam snorting out of his nostrils had a distinctly sulfurous tint in both color and stench.

"Whatever, Ramrodder," Scalped Hunter broke in before Ramrodder could draw down on Skunk Beansworth and reduce the size of the posse before they even got started. "What's yer idea fer catchin' this here Injun?"

It took visible effort for Ramrodder to get control of himself, but his eyes reverted to their normal bloodshot condition and the steam from his nostrils became noticably less sulphurous in both color and stench.

Finally, he looked down and kicked the dirt. "Ah shucks," he drawled. "Ah kind'a thunk mebbe one'a you would have an idea how t' do it."

That was when the Zinni Injun Red Fork Wathahiya stepped out of the shadows where he'd stood observing and listening in his inscrutable Indian manner and said, "Me know how track 'im."

Everybody turned and stared at the unexpected apparition with his arms folded across his chest and a tomahawk dangling deadly from his belt. There were hushed murmurs of, "An Injun?" The scalped part of Scalped Hunter's head began bleeding at the sight of the Injun.

"Why not an Injun!" Catastrophy Annie screeched. "Gen'l Custer uses Crow Injuns t' track down the Sioux and Cheyenne all the time."

"Yeah, 'n look where it got 'im!" someone shouted out. It was the August 4, 1876, and everybody knew what had happened at the Little Big Horn just a month earlier (though it seemed Catastrophy Annie didn't know).

People started turning angry faces toward Red Fork Wathahiya.

The red man showed no fear. He unfolded his arms and raised one hand. "The Injun who comes to burn your wikkiups is Yeechiphooie. Yeechiphooie Anazinnijo heap-bad medicine. Long before pale eyes come, Yeechiphooie master-god of all Anazinnijo, keep Anazinnijo as slaves. Anazinnijo fight long time, finally drive Yeechiphooie into underground and all Anazinnijo live free until pale eyes come, turn Anazinnijo into Zinni shepherds, blanket weavers, and quaint native American dancers for entertainment of pale eye tourists, and Japanese tourists who go around bothering people to pose with them for little pictures and buy kimchi dolls Zinni import from Korea. Me Zinni, used to be Anazinnijo.

Me rather sell blankets and dance for pale eye tourists, pose for little pictures with Japanese tourists and sell them kimchi dolls than be slave to Yeechiphooie. So me help you."

"Well what about the rest of them Zinni Injuns, they gonna help?" Buzzard Bait Northrup demanded.

Red Fork Wathahiya shook his head. "Other Zinni too afraid of Yeechiphooie. Most packing up, moving to Florida, wrestle alligators, sell turquoise jewelry to pale eye tourists."

Young Cassandra Mather, daughter of Parson Mather, stepped forward and shrieked, "You go to your doom!" But nobody backed out of the posse.

So it was that twenty intrepid souls, including Catastrophy Annie and the Zinni Injun Red Fork Wathahiya, headed out in search of Yeechiphooie and, after two weeks, found themselves having spaghetti for breakfast. *Again.* And back to our story.

They were halfway through eating, some few happily devouring the spaghetti in red sauce, some even hungry enough they didn't care what they consumed, but most complaining about spaghetti *again,* when an eerie and most ominous fog swept in from nowhere. The members of the posse all stopped eating and everybody looked up, trying in vain to pierce the dense, cloying, suffocating fog. Suddenly a most hideous and hideously loud laugh sounded and madly rang and echoed manically off the surrounding spire rocks in such a chaotic manner that none of them could perceive from whence it came.

"That's him!" Thrown Shoe Hammerforge cried, his teeth chattering enough like a full Mariachi band of castanets to set a Spanish senorita dancing. "He's north of us!"

"Tain't never no north o' us," Scalped Hunter cried back, his scalped scalp beginning to bleed once more just from hearing the laugh of the demented Anazinnijo god.

"Sou'east!" roared Keel Hauled Moby, who'd had enough of being a seaman and retired to arid Arizona to get away from ships, the sea, and fog.

"Due west!" insisted Ace Up His Sleeve Beauregard.

"Ever'body git yer shootin' arns out 'n git ready fer 'im!" Rybekka Ramrodder bellowed over everybody else.

"Gimme yer plates if'n you wants them clean fer lunch!" Cookie blabbered. He scampered about collecting the tin plates from everybody, and his attendant cloud of flies briefly left their station before his face and beard to aid him in cleaning off the tin plates that he gathered.

Silence thudded like twenty bales of

freshly plucked cotton boles over the overnight camp of the posse, except for the clicking and clacking of the cow-pokers, card-barracudas, and back-shooters checking their arsenal of deadly weaponry to make sure every-thing was loaded and ready to blaze out with the balefire that would send Yeechiphooie back to whatever Dante-an level of the ever-lasting inferno he come from.

Mad Cow Brazos opened the cylinder of his Navy Model 61 and critically eyed its loads. Satisfied that the primers good and were snugged firmly against the casing of his silver bul-lets, he snicked the cylin-der closed and peered deep into the fog, which was so dense he couldn't see the front sight of the pistol he held arm's length in front of himself.

Hung Dawg Hooligan checked the points on the miniature stake (guaran-teed to kill, or at least stop dead in his tracks, any vampire) in the chamber of his Henry, and put three more where he could grab them rapidly and reload, while Rybekka Ramrodder opened his Colt Junior Ca-det, saw the glow, and quietly closed it again, only to be asked by Skunk Beansworth: "What in tarnation is that green glow, Rebecca?"

RED FORK WATHAHIYA

"Don't call me Rebecca!" Ramrodder roared, the sulfurous steam from his nostrils only served to reduce the visi-bility in his vicinity to a foot and a half. But before he could say anything more a chorus of muffled *shhh!*s came at him through the creeping, crawling, itching fog.

"Whatever," Beansworth whispered. "What's the green glow?"

"It's called kryptonite," Rybecca Ram-rodder whispered harshly back.

"Wha's kryptonite?"

"Donno. It's green and it glows, and it's supposed to be able to stop super men daid in their tracks."

"Zat so? Well, I'll be. 'N here all I got fer my Sharps is holy water capsules, blest by the holy pope in Rome his own self."

"I keep telling ya, it's my oil of vitriol that's gonna do in that Yeechiphooie critter," came Cookie's voice as from an impossible distance as though he was being hauled away to a greater distance than they could imagine by some mon-ster none of them wished to think about.

The hideous and hid-eously loud laugh came again accompanied by a mighty wind that swept the fog away, only to blow up so much dust and sand they had to close their eyes, though most of them didn't get their eyes closed fast enough to keep from getting grit stuck painfully under their eyelids.

The wind stopped as suddenly as it began and they heard a **THUNK!** like the cleaver of the devil's own headsman chopping through a neck into a chopping block.

As soon as the intrepid members of the posse could clear out their eyes they looked at the chuck wagon to see a six-foot-long arrow quivering in its side.

"Oh, no you don't!" Cookie screamed. He bounded out from his hiding place under the chuck wagon and latched both hands firmly on the shaft of the mighty magical arrow and yanked. The quivering arrow jerked him off his feet. When he got his balance back, he spat on his hands, wiped them vigorously on the seat of his canvas pants, and grabbed the arrow again. This time his cloud of flies gave him a hand, and he managed to extract the arrow a bare instant before it burst into a sun-rivaling blaze of fire.

"YOW!" Cookie screamed, dancing like the whole Hole in the Wall Gang was shooting at his feet, and waving his hands around to kill the flames, but to no avail as while his hands were surely burned they just as sure weren't burning!

The hideous and hideously loud bedlam laugh of the insane Zinni god came again, and this time there was no confusion where it was, it was directly beneath a massive thunderstorm cloud closing in on them faster than they'd ever seen a cloud move before. Lightning shot down from the cloud, lighting up Yeechiphooie like a mysterious machine used by mad scientists trying to animate parts of dead bodies sewn together in awkward simulacrum of a person, followed almost immediately by a roll of thunder that knocked Cookie off his feet, as it did Catastrophy Annie and Buzzard Bait Northrop, who were speeding to the aid of the posse's cook.

Yeechiphooie laughed his hideous laugh once more and vanished from mortal sight.

Before anyone in the posse could even blink in wonder at the magical Injun god's vanishment the storm was upon them in all its fury. It was most fortunate none of them had pitched tents, if they had they would have had to spend days riding over half the Arizona Territory trying to find and retrieve their blown away shelters. As it was, the only thing that saved the chuck wagon from being tumbled away by the mighty wind was the weight of the barrels labeled "Flour" but which in fact contained nothing but the red sauce that Cookie cooked with the spaghetti from the barrels labeled "Pinto and Great Northern Beans."

The storm lasted only minutes, which was *very* fortunate, as the rain dropped so much water so fast that the cow-pokers, card-barracudas, and back-shooters were all completely soaked through. So much water came down from the sky that none of it had time to soak into the hardpan dirt before more came down, and the water that sluiced across the landscape was rapidly deepening until, by the time the storm stopped after only minutes of deluge, the water was already more than ankle deep and sweeping away anything not heavy enough to resist the flood water's force.

By the time the last of the flood dribbled away or percolated into the hardpan, and the posse rounded up everything important that had the waters had swept away, it was lunch time.

"Jeller!" Mad Cow Brazos bellowed. "Jeller fer lunch? *AGIN!*"

"Gotta have the jeller," Cookie bellowed right back at him. "All that carnsarned rain got into the barrels labled 'bacon' and wetted the jeller powder. So's we gotta eat it now b'fore it goes bad."

"Out'n mah way, Mad Cow," Hung Dawg Hooligan snarled. "Ah'm hungered som'pin fierce." He elbowed his way in front of Cookie and got his tin plate filled to the brim with red jeller with slices of cactus pear.

"Me like 'um jeller," Red Fork Wathahiya said from his place in line. "Look like blood. Taste like blood. Me like 'um." Scorpion Stung Shaunessey and Buffalo Apple Cranston, who stood to Wathahiya's sides in the chuck line, edged away from the Injun.

The cow-pokers, card-barracudas, and back-shooters of the posse grumbled, but ate their jeller, relieved that with the jeller powder wet they wouldn't have to eat much more of it.

When they finished eating Red Fork Wathahiya stood and solemnly intoned, "Me Yeechiphooie went."

"Take us there," Rybekka Ramrodder snarled.

The lone Zinni Injun helping the posse pointed at a distant mountain. "There," he said in a voice that tolled of doom.

It took a day's hard riding for the posse to reach the foot of the mountain where Wathahiya showed them the entrance of a cave and told them that was where Yeechiphooie went.

"Why couldn't you brung us heah sooner?" Rybekka Ramrodder demanded.

"Me knew Yeechiphooie not home until now," Red Fork replied haughtily.

"Why you . . ." Buzzard Bait Northrop snarled and advanced on the red man with his hands balled into fists.

Sidewinder Calhoun, Scorpion Stung Shaunessey, and Buffalo Apple Cranston, blood in their eyes, loosened their shooting irons in their holsters and joined Buzzard Bait Northrop in closing on the Injun.

"Now you jest stop right there!" Catastrophy Annie shrilled, stepping in front of Wathahiya. She wagged a finger in the manner of a schoolmarm scolding recalcitrant boys in the faces of the cow-pokers and back-shooters bent on doing the Zinni bodily harm and chided them severely.

"If'n it wasn't fer Red Fork heah, we wun't even know what we was up again', much less where t' find it!" she shrilled. "Now you jist *back* off 'n go 'bout yer business, 'n we'll git that there Yee-chiphooie. 'N that'll be thanks to this brave Injun here!"

RYBEKKA RAMRODDER

Buzzard Bait Northrop unclenched his fists and looked down sheepishly, and Sidewinder Calhoun, Scorpion Stung Shaunessey, and Buffalo Apple Cranston did their best to look like they weren't following him.

"Ain't no purpose going inta that cave now," Rybekka Ramrodder announced. "Let's chuck down, git a good night sleep, and we'll go in t' the cave in the mornin'." A chorus of agreement greeted the declairation.

"Chuck's ready!" Cookie shouted.

"Spaghetti!" Mad Cow Brazos roared when he saw the stringy, red-coated glop Cookie ladled into his tin plate.

"With a side o' jeller," Cookie said, slopping red jeller laced with tiny bits of a gila monster he'd just caught, killed, and gutted on top of the spaghetti in Mad Cow's tin dish. "Gotta git the jeller et while it kin still *be* et."

In the morning Rybekka Ramrodder distributed two pitch-headed torches to each of the seventeen who would enter the cave. He made Cookie stay outside with the chuck wagon over Cookie's protests, "Ah tell ya, it's mah oil of vitriol that'll do in thet Yeechiphooie!" Ramrodder also made Catastrophy Annie stay out, even though she insisted she was *more* able than any of the men were when he said she was too delicate to face the unknown horrors of the cave. Rybekka wasn't at all happy about leaving another man outside, but since Scalped Hunter's scalped scalp started bleeding again at the prospect of entering the Injun cave, he decided to have him stay outside to guard Catastrophy Annie and Cookie.

Scalped Hunter didn't argue the point at all.

"Light up ONE torch," Ramrodder ordered the sixteen cow-pokers, card-barracudas, back-shooters, and Red Fork Wathahiya, " 'n keep yer other un fer when the first un burns out." They lined up at Cookie's cook fire and each lit only one torch under Rybekka's watchful eye.

Inside the cave, the flickering torches

threw eerily dancing shadows over the rivuletted walls and floor of the caves.

"What in tarnation's thet?" Polecat Asskroft yelped when his torch lit up a scene of cabalistic Injun stick figures painted on the wall. The unsteady light of the torches made the stick figures seem to dance a wild and wooly war dance.

"Ugh," Red Fork Wathahiya rumbled when he pushed through the crowd to see what caught Polecat Asskroft's attention. "That heap old Anazinnijo med'cine. That chant-dance of Anazinnijo warriors, come drive Yeechiphooie deep inta cave. It work, too, Yeechiphooie not come back out for lo! these many moons from long time before pale eyes come."

Rybekka peered at the seemingly dancing stick figures, then looked suspiciously at Wathahiya. "Does that mean *we* gotta dance like 'em?"

The noble Zinni shook his head. "Dance only work for Anazinnijo. Pale eyes try that dance, it make Yeechiphooie stronger."

Relieved, Rybekka wiped nervous sweat from his forehead in relief, he wasn't a good dancer and didn't want to try to follow the complicated steps of the stick figures.

Their footsteps echoed hollowly as the seventeen continued into the depths of the cave, feeling with each step that they were descending ever deeper into the bowels of the Earth and if they kept going would eventually emerge blackened and wasted in China all the way on the other side of the world. They didn't go that far, though, before a hideous laugh even more hideously loud than any they had heard before stopped them, frozen to their cores with fear. Far ahead in the depths of the cave a faint glow appeared and slowly grew in size and brightness. After what felt like an eternity but in reality was less than an hour, the light was so bright it drowned out the glow of their torches — and in the middle of the light

stood the ten-foot-tall Injun god Yeechiphooie! He had a quiver of six-foot-long arrows slung over his shoulder and a eight-foot-long bow in his hand.

Laughing a dementedly manic and hideous laugh Yeechiphooie drew an arrow, fitted it to his bow, and aimed it straight into the posse!

That was enough for them.

"RUN!" screamed Skunk Beansworth. "Rebecca, make 'em run afore we's all kilt!"

"Don't call me Rebecca!" Rybecca Ramrodder roared and his roar was enough to jar the cow-pokers, card-barracudas, and back-shooters out of their unholy paralysis and start them running out of the cave. In their haste, they bowled Ramrodder over before his eyes turned full hellfire red and his snorting breath turned sulferous in both color and stench.

The leader of the posse leaped to his feet and followed the others out. All except Red Fork Wathahiya, the only man willing to stand and face the reincarnated Yeechiphooie.

Wathahiya began shuffling his feet and waving his arms in mimicry of the dancing feet of the Anazinnijo stick figures painted on the walls. His dancing worked for a time, and Yeechiphooie backed away, hiding his eyes behind his bent bow arm. But the evil god fought back until he was able to burst out with that hideous and hideously loud laugh. He gained strength and was able to stop backing away and hiding his eyes.

"Puny Anazinnijo brave," Yeechiphooie sneered. "You are strong, but one Anazinnijo brave is not enough to fend off the wrath of Yeechiphooie!" And he nocked the arrow he'd earlier drawn, drew his bow back, and let fly. The six-foot-long arrow flew straight and true and struck Red Fork Wathahiya in the center of his breastbone, as though a bullseye had been drawn on the spot, and drove him back, skewering the noble savage flat against the cave wall in the midst of the dancing Anazinnijo stick figures. Then the ancient, evil god pranced after the hastily departed posse.

There was a great clangoring and thudding at the mouth of the cave when the cow-pokers, card-barracudas, and back-shooters of the posse ran smack dab straight into the chuck wagon which Cookie, helped by Catastrophy Annie and Scalped Hunter had moved there.

"Careful there!" Cookie screamed. "Don't spill the oil of vitriol!"

"What in tarnation's goin' on heah?" Rybekka Ramrodder demanded when he made it to the mouth of the cave and saw the posse untangling itself and struggling to their feet.

"Dang people came crashing right out o' the cage 'thout looking where they was goin' and ran smack dab straight inta the trap Ah dun set fer that Injun god!" Cookie exclaimed.

Ramrodder looked at the chuck wagon stretched across the mouth of the cave and at the two barrels of oil of vitriol that perched precariously on its top and shook his head in wonder. "Do ya really think that'll work?" he asked.

Cookie looked at the people still unheaping themselves, listened to the approaching prance of Yeechiphooie, and said, "It better or we's in big trouble. Now hep me git these people out'n the way!"

Rybekka Ramrodder pitched in and they had everyone cleared out of the way right before Yeechiphooie switched from a prance to a charge and roared out of the cave — smack dab straight into the chuck wagon.

A charging ten-foot-tall evil Anazinnijo god carries a humungous amount of momentum, and Yeechiphooie's mo-

mentum was enough to dislodge the barrels of oil of vitriol from their unsteady perch atop the chuck wagon, and they crashed down, dumping their contents on the reincarnated god.

The immortal Yeechiphooie screamed in mortal agony when the oil of vitriol slopped over his body. He swiped at it with his hands in futile attempt to brush it away, but every swipe of his huge hands merely served to spread the deadly oil further onto untouched parts of his body.

Steam rose where the bubbling oil of vitriol ate at his flesh, turning it into molten gunk that dripped and spattered to the rocky ground. In moments, all that was left of Yeechiphooie was his gurgling scream, and even that didn't last much longer.

There was silence for a time as the cow-pokers, card-barracudas, and back-shooters looked at the unholy and sickly mess on the rocks where the terror of West Archaic had just met his grisly demise.

"Whar's Red Fork Wathahiya?" Catastrophy Annie finally asked. "We owe him a big thanks. And Cookie, too."

Rybekka Ramrodder looked at the cave entrance, and the spreading puddle of gunk in front of it that he knew no man could cross alive and said, "I heard him dancin' that Anazinnijo dance b'hind me. I think he died givin' the rest o' us time ta git out'n the cave."

"We'll put up a memorial ta him in the town square," Buzzard Bait Northrop said, wiping a tear from his eye."

"Ta him and ta Cookie," Mad Cow Brazos said, draping an arm over Cookie's shoulder.

And so the town of West Archaic was saved from the evil Anazinnijo god Yeechiphooie.

DRY DAYS IN YELLOW GULCH

by John Gregory Betancourt

Author of "Spectres of Yellow Gulch," "Demon Steers of Yellow Gulch," etc.

illustrated by P. d' Omaine

"Jumpin' coyotes!" Bronx gave a whistle, twisting in his saddle to look around at all the empty buildings. Windows gaped, their glass broken out. Doors stood open. A pair of tumbleweeds rolled past. A desolate wind moaned. Lonely coyotes barked in the distance.

Something was wrong in Yellow Gulch, but he couldn't quite put his finger on it.

"Ghost town," came the Old Man's gravelly voice.

"G-ghosts, suh?" Bronx glanced sidelong at his friend, who merely hawked and spat into the dust.

"Yup," the Old Man said. "I seen it before. Happens when a town goes dry."

"Dry." Bronx's brow furrowed. That meant something bad.

"The alcohol springs musta played out while we was in Mexico. No wonder folks skee-daddled."

"Oh no!" Bronx swallowed hard. He had been looking forward to a tall beer in the saloon. It sounded like he wouldn't get one now.

Their palominos seemed to recognize Yellow Gulch. Though they had been away two long months on a cattle drive, both horses halted at the hitching rail in front of the Scarlet Lady Saloon.

"I need a drink," Bronx said. He had six silver dollars jingling in his pocket — the remains of two months' wages.

"The town's gone dry, Bronx," the Old Man reminded him patiently.

"Oh." Bronx's brow furrowed. That meant something bad. What was it again?

"Yup," said the Old Man. "Alcohol springs're gone. Remember?"

"Oh." Bronx felt near to crying. No beer, then!

As they dismounted, Big Betty, the owner of the Scarlet Lady, pushed open the swinging doors and stared down at them. At six feet tall, dressed in a bright red teddy and black fishnet stockings, she towered over Bronx and the Old Man. Big Betty had obviously been crying. Long black mascara trails ran from her eyes, which were pink and puffy.

"Is she a ghost?" Bronx asked softly.

"Shut up and show some respect for a lady," whispered the Old Man. He took off his hat. "Good day, Miss Betty," he added, slicking back his hair with one hand.

Bronx doffed his Stetson. He liked ladies. Especially big ones.

"Howdy, boys," Big Betty rasped, sounding like a pale shadow of her former self. "What can I get y'all today?"

"Beer, ma'am," said Bronx.

"A bath," said the Old Man.

"Water we got aplenty. For your horses, too. Beer, though . . ." She gave a little sob. "We've gone dry as the bones of a camel that's lain in the Great Gobi Desert for a year and a day! Twice as dry!"

"How'd it happen, Betty?" asked the Old Man. "Anything we can do to help?"

"Well . . ." She licked her lips, and suddenly her gaze grew thoughtful.

"You boys any good with those guns you-all are totin'?"

"The kid ain't never been beat," said the Old Man proudly. "Me, I'm an explosives man, m'self. Don't do no gun-slingin'."

Bronx grinned up at Betty. She had pretty white globes pushing up from the front of her teddy, and he thought he'd like to touch them.

"He's fast?" Big Betty asked.

"I rent my women by the *minute!*" Bronx said proudly.

"Fast *with a gun?*" she asked.

Bronx scratched his head, puzzled. "Never tried with a gun," he said. "The barrel's a little small for my —"

"The kid ain't too smart," the Old Man said quickly. "But his heart's in the right place. Put a six-shooter in his hand, face him the right direction, and stand back. He'll blast everything in sight."

Bronx brightened. "Yep!" Blasting things he understood.

As Betty stared appraisingly at him, Bronx drew his pistol like greased lightning, then smoothly reversed it to show off the handle. More than two dozen notches had been carved into the ivory.

"Look!" he said, pointing. "I got me a dozen Injuns, two outlaws, a Yankee, and fourteen armadillos!"

"Armadillos?" Betty asked the Old Man.

He shrugged. "The kid's got a thing about 'em," he said apologetically. "T'ain't nothing I can do about it. Musta been skeered by one as a babe."

"That's a mite odd," she said.

The Old Man shrugged. "The kid's all right," he said. "I've known him since he was knee-high to a goat. Since his parents died, I've kinda looked out for him. Kept him on the straight and narrow, as the Good Book says. Saved his life more times than I can count. He'd be lost without me."

"Come on in, boys," Big Betty said. "Let's talk. Maybe you *can* help me."

It turned out Big Betty was the last person left in Yellow Gulch. Everyone else had left. Bronx and the Old Man sat at a table in the saloon, surrounded by now-silent roulette wheels, blackjack tables, and other gambling devices. Betty went over to the long and dusty mahogany bar, reached behind it with a knowing wink, and pulled out three shot glasses and a small stoppered bottle.

"What's that?" Bronx asked, licking his lips. It *looked* like something mighty good to drink.

"It ain't water, son!" she said with a laugh. She pulled the cork with her teeth, poured out the last of the contents into the shot glasses, and flung the bottle over her shoulder. It sailed out an open window. Then she spat the cork into a spitoon. "You-all are gazin' at the last alcohol in all of Yellow Gulch. I been savin' it for a special occasion."

"Thanks," Bronx said, wiping the back of his sleeve across his mouth. "I needed three drinks!"

"What — how — ?" Big Betty sputtered, staring down at the three suddenly empty shot glasses.

"Told you he was fast," the Old Man said. "Have to watch your fingers at chow time."

"Honey," Big Betty said, putting at arm around Bronx's shoulders.

He smelled her perfume, sweet and exotic.

"If you can get rid of them scalawags what made off with Yellow Gulch's alcohol supply, you got free drinks here for life!"

"And women?" Bronx asked eagerly.

"How's about five minutes free per day!"

"Wee—hoo," Bronx yodeled triumphantly. "Time to spare fer cuddlin'!"

"Before you get to sparkin' on those 'maginary gals," the Old Man said to Bronx, "let's find out what we're up against."

Big Betty began to talk fast and earnestly with the Old Man. Something about slantwise pipelines being drilled from Digsby, the next town over, hitting the motherlode of alcohol lying under Yellow Gulch. Bronx's eyes glazed over as she talked about powerful pumps sucking out the beer and whiskey faster than Mother Nature could refill the underground reservoirs. Yellow Gulch's wells didn't go deep enough to reach what little alcohol remained.

"Got it!" the Old Man said. He rose and hitched up his britches. "We'll water our horses, then head on out for Digsby. Comin' Bronx?"

"Yes, suh!" Bronx was on his feet fast as you please. He flashed Big Betty a wide grin and headed for the door, his thoughts turning to the five minutes a day (not to mention unlimited beer) that Big Betty had promised.

The three-mile ride to Digsby didn't take long, and they arrived at suppertime. Here was a real boomtown, Bronx thought, staring wide-eyed at the bustle. Buildings were going up fast in all directions, dozens of them. Men and women packed the streets. Children and dogs darted through the crowds,

F. Domain

laughing and playing. Horses and wagons came and went in a steady stream. As they watched, a pair of stagecoaches pulled to a stop in front of Carson's Dry Goods and began unloading passengers. Yes, Digsby was certainly the place to be right now.

Bronx and the Old Man swung down from their saddles and led their palominos forward. Bronx eyed the women, but none seemed the least bit interested in cuddling up with him for the night. Well, maybe he'd find one at the saloon. He still had those six silver dollars jingling in his pocket . . .

Suddenly, the Old Man nudged Bronx, indicating a dozen or so buckboard wagons lined up at the side entrance to a large building. A half dozen men rolled barrels marked **BEER** and **XXX** out the door, up a ramp, and onto the nearest wagon.

"What's the sign say, suh?" Bronx asked. He wished he could read.

"That's the town hall. They musta drilled to Yellow Gulch from there," the Old Man whispered, "straight to the alcohol."

The barrels reminded Bronx of something. What? His brow furrowed. Oh yes — he was dry from the ride. Three little shots an hour back hadn't slaked his thirst one bit.

"How about a beer, suh?" he asked, licking his lips.

The Old Man nodded. "Couldn't hurt. Bet we can learn a mite more in the saloon, too!"

The Crazy Lady Saloon was packed, just like the rest of Digsby. It took a couple minutes for spots to open up at the bar. They bellied up and Bronx slapped a silver dollar down.

"Beer for me an' my pal!" he called loudly.

Seconds later, a thin-faced bartender with a handlebar mustache whizzed two tall frothy mugs their way, plus ninety cents in shiny silver dimes.

"Here ya go, son."

"Thanks. The name's Bronx."

"Broncs? Like the horses?"

"Nah," said the Old Man with a chuckle, leaning in. "Bronx, like in New York out east."

"He ain't got that Eastern accent."

"I ain't never been east of the Mississississis . . ." Bronx trailed off. "Missis Ississy . . . Miss . . ."

"The big river," said the Old Man patiently.

"That's the one!" said Bronx.

The bartender scratched his head. "Then why call him Bronx — ?" he began.

The Old Man chuckled. "He used to be called Tex. But when we worked for Tex Wheeler out at the Big Wheel Ranch, there were four other hands named Tex, so we all got to calling the kid Bronx, just to tell him from the others."

"Five *Tex*es made for a powerful confusion," Bronx admitted.

The bartender chuckled. "I can understand that. Say, Bronx, why not try your luck at the wheel?" he added with a knowing wink and a nod toward the roulette table. "You look lucky." He moved on to wait on another customer.

"I do?" Bronx looked at the Old Man. "I look lucky!"

"Lucky for *them*, he means," said the Old Man softly. "That wheel will take all your money. Stay away from it."

Bronx frowned. He didn't like losing money, not one bit.

"Should I shoot that varmint?" he asked in a low voice, nodding toward the bartender. His fingers itched for his gun.

The Old Man chuckled. "Save your bullets for tonight. We have to save Big Betty and Yellow Gulch, remember."

"Yes, suh!"

Bronx commenced to sipping his beer and glaring over the rim of his mug at the bartender.

Beside him, the Old Man struck up a conversation with other drinkers. Was their honest work in Digsby? Yes, they

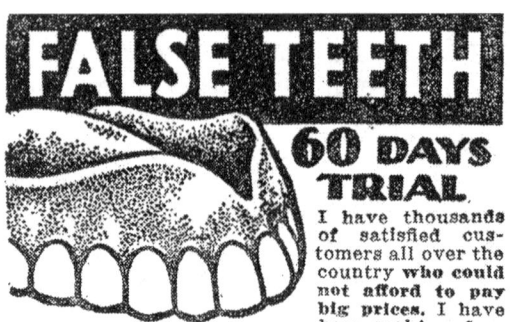

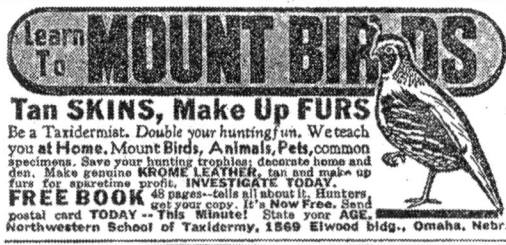

were usually hiring at the Town Hall. What sort of work? All sorts in the alcohol trade. Who's hiring? Just ask a red-bearded gent named Rusty Moore. It seemed the mayor of Digsby had been drilling, and sure enough he hit the motherlode of beer and whiskey reserves.

"Suh?" Bronx tugged at the Old Man's sleeve.

"What is it?" he asked in a kindly voice.

"Are we going to work for them varmints?" Bronx asked. "I thought —"

"Let me do the thinking, Bronx. Have yourself another beer."

Bronx shrugged. "Yes, suh." He drained his mug fast, slammed it down, then slid a shiny silver dime toward the bartender. "Two more here!" he called. He still had a powerful thirst.

Ten minutes later, the Old Man slapped his back. "I think we know enough now," he said.

"Know what, suh?" Bronx asked, looking up from the line of ten empty mugs before him. His tongue felt thick; words came out slow and slurry.

"About the drillin', of course!"

Bronx shrugged. "Okay." He was in too good a mood to ask questions right now. All that beer sat pretty well in his belly, if he did say so himself. Which he did.

"I don't know about you," said the Old Man with a grin, "but I'm ready for a good night's work."

"Huh!" said Bronx. "We're done work-

in' for a while, 'member?" He jingled his five silver dollars and four remaining dimes. "Got money enough for a *lot* of beer!"

"Not the way *you* drink it!"

Bronx frowned, then grinned. That had to be a joke.

The Old Man led the way out to the street. They got their horses, took them to the livery stable, and left them there for the night. Bronx saw the Old Man whisk several things from the saddle-bags into his pocket. After that, they went back to the street, waited for a break in the passing line of wagons, then trotted across to the town hall. Bronx wobbled after him. What was the rush? All of Digsby looked mighty fine right now, bathed in the sunset's glow. In his opinion, what they needed was more alcohol, a couple of long baths, and some of those bee-*yoo*-tee-full saloon gals. But the Old Man was in charge, and one thing Bronx had learned was to always do what the Old Man said.

Bronx trailed him around to the side of the town hall, where men continued to roll barrels out the door, up a ramp, and into waiting wagons. The two of them stood side by side, watching.

Finally a short, burly man with a thick red beard took notice. He squinted at Bronx, then the Old Man, then frowned.

"What're you two lookin' at?" he demanded. "Sheriff don't allow no loiterin' hereabouts. So git!"

Bronx felt a cold wind touch him. His fingers itched and moved subtly toward his pistol. Suddenly the world got very, very clear and the burly man very, very large. Time for another notch? He glanced at the Old Man, hoping for the let-fly signal, but the Old Man just grinned up at the red-bearded stranger.

"We're lookin' for Rusty Moore," the Old Man drawled. "Just got into town. Heard he could use a few more hands. What do you say?"

Red-beard hesitated.

by John Gregory Betancourt

"Come on, Rusty!" one of the barrel-rollers called. "Ya know we're short-handed!"

"All right," Rusty snapped. He looked hard at Bronx and the Old Man, frowned, then gave a curt nod. "We'll try you for a shift. Get up here. Pay's thirty-five cents a day, plus all the beer you can drink."

"Sounds good to me!" Bronx said, licking his lips. More free beer!

"You drink off-shift at the saloon. Show up drunk for work, you're out. Got it?"

"Yes, sir, Mr. Moore!" said the Old Man cheerfully. Bronx saw the sharp look of a wolf in his smile. "Where do we begin?"

Bronx and the Old Man, along with six others on the night shift, spent the next few hours rolling barrels out to wagons. Bronx worked silently, his thoughts filled with dreams of free beer. The Old Man chatted amiably with the other men, and slowly Bronx started to get an idea of how things worked in Digsby.

The Town Hall had a pump in its basement bringing up the liquid gold. Brewmasters ran the alcoholic sludge through purifying filters on the first floor, separating beer from whiskey, then kegging both up for transport. Bronx, the Old Man, and the others on their shift rolled heavy barrels out to wagons bound for half the west — from San Francisco to the Arizona Territories and everywhere in between.

Finally Rusty signaled a break, and

F. Donsin

everyone sat on the Town Hall's steps to chew tobacco, drink cups of water, and rest. It must have been ten or eleven o'clock. The moon was full, and light spilled out from the saloon and half the businesses along the main street.

"Got to visit the outhouse," Bronx announced, rising.

With a yawn and a stretch, the Old Man said he'd go, too. So the pair of them trooped into the shadows at the rear of the Town Hall. There the Old Man slapped Bronx on the back.

"Good idea for a diversion!" he whispered.

"Suh?" said Bronx, puzzled.

But the Old Man was already pushing up one of the Town Hall's windows. Silent as a ghost, he slipped inside the dark room. With a puzzled shrug, Bronx followed.

It took a minute for Bronx's eyes to adjust to the near perfect darkness. Just enough moonlight streamed in for him to make out half a dozen desks covered with piles of paper. They sure seemed to have a lot of it.

"Must be orders for stolen booze," the Old Man whispered. He crept to the door, cracked it open, and peeked out. A blade of yellow lamplight highlighted his weather-lined face.

"Come on!" he said urgently. "It's clear!"

They both crept out into a long hallway. This was the spot from which they had been fetching beer and whiskey for the wagons; the floor was scuffed and scarred from rolling all the heavy barrels.

Softly they crept past open doors. The first held empty barrels, waiting to be filled. The second held giant vats attached to each other by long coiled pipes. The vats bubbled and hissed. A man wearing the leather apron of a brewmaster sat at a table inside, smoking a cigar and playing solitaire. He didn't so much as glanced up as Bronx and the Old Man eased by.

At the end of the hall, the two of them

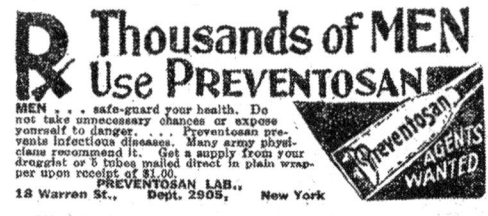
came to a wide stairway leading down. The basement? Bronx heard an animal snort from below, and a man's low voice said, "Easy there, big fellow!"

"Must have mules down there for turnin' the pumps," the Old Man said. "Get ready!"

Quick as lightning, Bronx had his pistol drawn. The Old Man reached way down deep in his pockets and pulled out two sticks of dynamite. Then he chortled to himself. Bronx knew how the Old Man liked to blow things up, and he grinned, too.

"Ready, Bronx?" the Old Man asked.

"Yes, suh!"

"Then let's go!"

Side by side, they descended the stairs. At least one lantern glowed from somewhere down there. Bronx strained to hear and caught the *shup-shup* of hooves shifting in sawdust, followed by another low snort. Stable smells rose around him, thick and earthy; the place needed to be mucked out. It would be a shame to blow up poor dumb critters; maybe he could get the mules out before the blast . . .

The Old Man stopped suddenly.

"Suh?" Bronx whispered.

"Sh-h!" came the reply. Then, using Indian sign-language, he motioned for caution. Bronx nodded.

Then, together, they bent and peeked around the steps toward the center of the basement.

It had a dirt floor, of course, but sawdust an inch deep covered it most places. Thick wooden pillars supported large ceiling beams. Oil lanterns hung

from several of the beams, casting a smoky yellow glow over everything. Bronx stared at the nearest pillar — long pegs held strangely shaped leather harnesses and ropes.

The Old Man motioned bent double and zig-zagged toward the center of the basement. Then he came up short and peeked around a column. A second later, Bronx joined him.

A round path had been beaten into the floor just ahead, circling an animal-powered turn-pump. Two beasts could be tied to the pump at any one time, where they would march around and around in a circle, turning the giant screw that pulled alcohol from the depths of the Earth.

Bronx stared in awe at the massive pipe running up from the pump and through the ceiling-boards. That was where beer and whiskey came from!

Animal snorts came from ahead. Bronx managed to tear his gaze away from the pump. In the far corner of the basement sat a high wooden pen. A man was leaning on its top board, gazing at the animals within. Those had to be the mules.

The Old Man smiled his wolflike smile, then held up one finger. Using Indian sign-language again, he instructed Bronx to sneak up behind the man and knock him out.

Bronx nodded. Softly he crept down the steps and advanced on the mule-wrangler. The fellow continued to lean on the top board of the pen, watching his mules.

The animals must have heard or sensed Bronx's approach because they suddenly shifted and let out warning snorts. A head reared up over the pen, and beady black eyes stared straight into Bronx's.

Bronx let out a scream of, *"Armadillo!"* and let fly with his bullets.

Bam! Bam! Bam! He caught the giant beast square in the forehead, sending it flopping over backwards. *Bam! Bam! Bam!* More lead flew, catching the huge

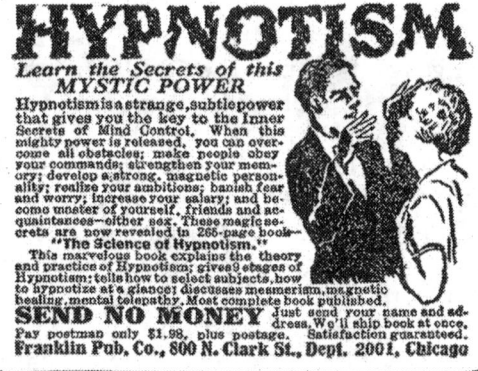

by John Gregory Betancourt

creature in the neck and side. It shuddered and lay still.

It was the biggest armadillo Bronx had ever seen before — taller than a man! — with scales and a long fanged snout. And there were more in the pen — half a dozen more! Each larger and more terrible than the last! Some had six legs, others had eight —

Bronx blinked and realized the man leaning on the fence had disappeared. Turning, he spotted the varmint running for the stairs like his tail was on fire. Dang it! Bronx raised his gun and pulled the trigger, but the hammer fell on an empty cylinder. He had used all his bullets on that giant armadillo!

The Old Man came running. "What's wrong, boy?" he demanded. "Why'd you let that varmint git away?"

"L-look!" Bronx pointed a shaking finger at the pen.

"What in —" the Old Man began, staring. Bronx saw the blood drain from his face.

"Armadillos, suh!" Bronx broke open his gun and rapidly reloaded. *Best to kill them all now. Didn't the Good Book say, 'Thou shalt not suffer an armadillo to live'?*

"I don't know what in blazes those things are," gasped the Old Man, "but I know those ain't armadillos! Leave 'em be, boy! We'll blow this place sky-high and send them unholy critters back to whatever hell they crawled from!"

The man who had escaped was already shouting for help at the top of the basement stairs. Bronx took a deep breath. Some things couldn't be helped. He'd have to shoot anyone who came down the basement steps. After all, he couldn't disappoint Big Betty.

The Old Man had pulled more sticks of dynamite from his pants pocket and inserted the detonator cap and the fuse. Bronx spotted two sticks already sitting on the turn-pump, and he left two more by the pen of armadillo-monsters.

"Got a match?" the Old Man asked.

"Yes, suh!" Bronx produced one and struck it with his thumb.

"Light it. I'll get the other."

"Yes, suh!"

Bronx bent and lit the fuse. It commenced to sparking and sputtering.

"We have two minutes to get out," the Old Man said.

Men were pounding down the steps to the basement. *Bam!* Bronx put a slug into the basement wall six inches from the first man's head. Yelping, he turned and high-tailed it back upstairs.

"Whoever's down there," came Rusty Moore's booming voice, "throw down your weapons and come out so we can lynch you!"

"Come get me!" Bronx shouted.

He fired another bullet when Rusty poked his head down to see what was happening. It took off the tip of Rusty's nose, and the overseer commenced to cussing a blue streak.

"One minute!" the Old Man said urgently. "We have to git out of here, boy, or we ain't going to make it! That dynamite is set to blow in a minute and a half!"

"Any ideas?" Bronx asked.

"Yes, but you ain't going to like it . . ."

"Tell me!" Bronx begged. He didn't want to die.

"We gotta ride them giant armadillos out of here, Bronx! They're big, and I bet they can clear us a path up the stairs!"

Bronx gaped. "Ride — !" he began.

"Yes! Hurry!" He ran for the pen.

"I — I can't!" Bronx cried.

"You have to!"

Bronx shuddered. He just couldn't.

"I'll follow you up!" he said. "Go!"

The Old Man shifted the latch and pulled the gate open. Blood pooled darkly around the giant armadillo-creature Bronx had killed. Five more huddled at the back of the pen. Two of them wore leather halters — ready to be hitched to the turn-pump.

"He-*yah!*" the Old Man shouted, running straight at them and waving his hat.

They panicked. First one, then another bolted from the pen. They headed past the pump for the stairs, as if sensing their freedom lay at hand.

The Old Man grabbed the last one's halter and swung up onto his back. Instead of tucking its head down and running faster, though, it started to buck like a horse being broken to the saddle.

The Old Man would have been fine if not for the wooden beams overhead. As Bronx watched, the bucking armadillo knocked the Old Man's head against the ceiling. He sagged and started to slide off.

"Yee-ha!" Bronx cried. The Old Man needed him!

Swallowing his fear, he leaped forward, grabbed hold of the Old Man with one hand and the halter with his other. He latched on hard with his knees, kicked with his heels, and turned the critter's head for the stairs.

The giant armadillos squealed and headed for the steps. Bronx risked a glance at the Old Man. Blood covered his forehead; his eyes were closed.

The other armadillos were milling around at the foot of the stairs. Half a dozen men stood there with guns drawn, blocking the way.

Bronx risked letting go of the halter and drew his gun. He started shooting, and at the loud *bam! bam! bam!* the other four armadillos decided it was time to leave.

They rushed the stairs. At the sight of the monstrous stampede, the men turned to flee — and fell screaming as huge clawed feet trampled over

by John Gregory Betancourt

them!

Bronx holstered his gun and urged his mount to the stairs. Up, up, and still up they raced, then down the hall. They burst out onto the ramp, leaped over the wagon waiting to be loaded, and kept on going into the darkness.

Bronx clung to his mount and the Old Man, nearly petrified with fear. Behind them, he heard a huge *whump!* of sound, followed by an explosion as the Town Hall blew up. A huge fire made the back of his head and arms grow hot. Then splinters of wood rained down, needling his skin.

They must have stung his mount something worse; squealing like a pig, it raced after the other armadillos into the darkness.

Long about sunrise, Bronx and the Old Man had their new steed figured out enough to steer it toward Yellow Gulch. Their giant armadillo-critter was not so bad, Bronx thought, reaching down and patting its neck. Not *quite* an armadillo. Maybe a second cousin twice removed. Just far enough away that he could tolerate it.

Luckily the Old Man had only been stunned from that blow to his head. Ten minutes out from Digsby, he was talking a blue streak. How they had saved Yellow Gulch. How Big Betty would be grateful forever. And how they would both enjoy their free beer for life at her saloon.

"You saved me!" the Old Man said, sounding shocked. "I can't believe . . . you saved me!"

Bronx grinned. "Yes, suh!"

He certainly looked forward to that beer!

It was dawn by the time they found their way back to Yellow Gulch. They set the big brute of an armadillo free on the outskirts of town, then walked down the main street toward the Scarlet Lady Saloon.

Big Betty was waiting for them in front of the Scarlet Lady Saloon. She wore her finest red teddy, black fishnet stockings, and a huge grin.

"They're back!" she yelled, stepping into the street. "They're back! They're back!"

People began pouring out from the storefronts and houses. Bronx stared at all the men and women in amazement. Where had they come from? There had to be fifty or more, and yesterday Yellow Gulch had been a ghost town.

The crowd gathered about them, laughing and grinning and calling welcomes. The men all seemed to want to pat Bronx and the Old Man on the back. Bronx just grinned and shrugged. Well, there were worse things in life!

"As soon as you left," Big Betty said, giving them both smothering hugs, "I sent telegrams to everyone and let them know our troubles would soon be over! The whole town is coming back! You saved Yellow Gulch!"

"The underground reservoirs have started filling up again," said a man in a tall black hat. He had a funny way of talking, fast and nasal, and his gray coat was long and entirely too clean.

"Who are you?" the Old Man asked him suspiciously.

"Sorry!" the man said with a quick smile. "I'm Nate Bridges, the geologist from Washington. You've done the citizens of Yellow Gulch a great service. According to my tests this morning, the town's alcohol supply will be back to normal within a week!"

"Wee—*hoo!*" Bronx shouted. He threw his hat into the air. Free beer for life!

The crowd clapped. Someone pressed a mug into Bronx's hand — "Imported just for this celebration," Big Betty whispered — and he raised it in a toast.

"To Big Betty!" he called.

Girls from the saloon were passing out free beer to everyone. Dozens of mugs went up, along with a cheer.

"To Big Betty!" the crowd called.

Betty gave Bronx a big wink. "Extra time f' cuddlin'," she reminded him.

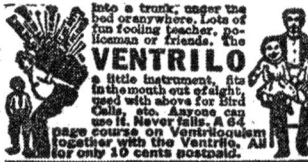

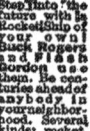
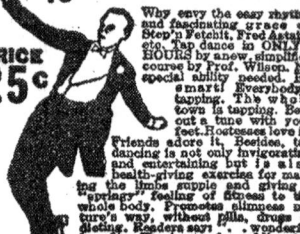

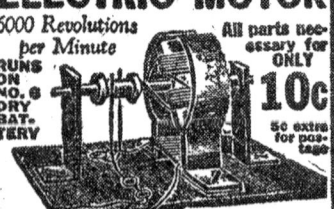
118

MAN AND WIFE WANTED!

To run local COFFEE AGENCY

Splendid Chance To Make Up To $60.00 in a Week

NEW FORDS
GIVEN AS A BONUS

If you are married and willing to cooperate with your life partner in operating a Coffee Agency right in your own locality, send your name at once for full details about my plan—FREE.

It is now possible for married couples to make up to $60 in a single week if you can work harmoniously together. Wife handles the orders, keeps records, etc., while the husband delivers and collects. Steady, permanent business of one to two hundred customers can quickly be established if you follow the simple, proven plans that I send.

START EARNING AT ONCE

I'll send you everything you need—your complete outfit containing full-size packages of products, also printed forms, blanks, advertising literature, samples, etc., together with simple instructions for both the husband and wife, so you can start your earnings right away. Make as high as $45.00 your very first week.

Everybody uses Coffee, Tea, Spices, Flavoring Extracts, Baking Powder, Flour, Cocoa, Canned Goods, and other foods every day. They MUST BUY these things to live. You simply take care of your regular customers right in your locality—just keep them supplied with the things they need. You handle all the money and pocket a big share of it for yourself. You keep all the profits—you don't divide up with anyone. Hundreds of housewives in many localities are waiting, right now, to be served with these nationally famous products.

I SEND EVERYTHING

Just as soon as I hear from you I will send you complete details—tell you all the inside workings of this nation-wide Coffee Agency Plan. I will explain just how to establish your customers: how to give them service and make good cash earnings. You can plan it so you give only 5 days a week to your business, collect your profits on Friday, and have all day Saturday and Sunday for vacation or rest. The plans I send you took years to perfect. You know they must be good because they have brought quick help to hundreds of other men and women, both married and single, who needed money.

FORD CARS GIVEN

Over and above the cash earnings you make I will give you a brand-new Ford Sedan as a bonus for producing. This is not a contest or a raffle. I offer a Ford Car—as an extra reward—to everyone who starts in this business.

YOU DON'T RISK A PENNY

You can start a Coffee Agency and make money the first week. You don't have to risk a cent of your own money. I absolutely guarantee this. No experience is needed. You use your home as headquarters. You can build your business on our capital. Full details of money making plans are free. Send your name today for the free book giving all inside facts, then you can decide. Don't waste a minute as you might lose this opportunity through the unnecessary delay. ACT AT ONCE.

ALBERT MILLS,
3714 Monmouth Ave.,   **Cincinnati, Ohio**

WONDERFUL SUCCESS

Reported by Others
+

Clare C. Wellman, N. J., tried my plan and cleared $96.00 in a week. Hans Coordes, Nebr., made $27.95 in a day; $96.40 in a week. Norman Geisler, Mich., reported $33.00 profit for one day and as high as $129.00 in a single week. Ruby Hannen, a woman in West Virginia, stated that she made $17.00 in one day and $73.00 in a week. Wilbur Whitcomb, Ohio, reported $30.00 profit in a day and $146.00 in one week. I have scores of reports of exceptional earnings like these as evidence of the amazing possibilities of this money-making offer.

Free Offer COUPON

ALBERT MILLS, President
3714 Monmouth Ave., Cincinnati, Ohio

Send your free book telling how to start a local Coffee Agency in which a married couple (or single persons) can make up to $60.00 in a week. We will read it and then let you know if we want to accept this opportunity.

Name...

Address..

....
(Please Print or Write Plainly)

www.ingramcontent.com/pod-product-compliance
Lightning Source LLC
Chambersburg PA
CBHW080825020726
47501CB00009B/2429

* 9 7 8 0 8 0 9 5 1 1 5 0 1 *